Books by Shirleen Davies

Historical Western Romance Series
Redemption Mountain

Redemption's Edge, Book One
Wildfire Creek, Book Two
Sunrise Ridge, Book Three
Dixie Moon, Book Four
Survivor Pass, Book Five
Promise Trail, Book Six
Deep River, Book Seven
Courage Canyon, Book Eight
Forsaken Falls, Book Nine
Solitude Gorge, Book Ten
Rogue Rapids, Book Eleven
Angel Peak, Book Twelve
Restless Wind, Book Thirteen
Storm Summit, Book Fourteen
Mystery Mesa, Book Fifteen
Thunder Valley, Book Sixteen
A Very Splendor Christmas, Holiday Novella, Book Seventeen
Paradise Point, Book Eighteen,
Silent Sunset, Book Nineteen, Coming Next in the Series!

MacLarens of Boundary Mountain

Colin's Quest, Book One,
Brodie's Gamble, Book Two
Quinn's Honor, Book Three

Sam's Legacy, Book Four
Heather's Choice, Book Five
Nate's Destiny, Book Six
Blaine's Wager, Book Seven
Fletcher's Pride, Book Eight
Bay's Desire, Book Nine
Cam's Hope, Book Ten

MacLarens of Fire Mountain

Tougher than the Rest, Book One
Faster than the Rest, Book Two
Harder than the Rest, Book Three
Stronger than the Rest, Book Four
Deadlier than the Rest, Book Five
Wilder than the Rest, Book Six

Romantic Suspense

Eternal Brethren, Military Romantic Suspense

Steadfast, Book One
Shattered, Book Two
Haunted, Book Three
Untamed, Book Four
Devoted, Book Five
Faithful, Book Six
Exposed, Book Seven
Undaunted, Book Eight
Resolute, Book Nine

Unspoken, Book Ten, Coming Next in the Series!

Peregrine Bay, Romantic Suspense

Reclaiming Love, Book One
Our Kind of Love, Book Two
Edge of Love, Book Three, Coming Next in the Series!

Contemporary Romance Series

MacLarens of Fire Mountain

Second Summer, Book One
Hard Landing, Book Two
One More Day, Book Three
All Your Nights, Book Four
Always Love You, Book Five
Hearts Don't Lie, Book Six
No Getting Over You, Book Seven
'Til the Sun Comes Up, Book Eight
Foolish Heart, Book Nine

Macklin's of Burnt River

Thorn's Journey
Del's Choice
Boone's Surrender

The best way to stay in touch is to subscribe to my newsletter. Go to https://www.shirleendavies.com/ and subscribe in the box at the top of the right column that asks for your email. You'll be notified of new books before they are released, have chances to win great prizes, and receive other subscriber-only specials.

Paradise Point

Redemption Mountain Historical Western Romance Series

SHIRLEEN DAVIES

Book Eighteen in the Redemption Mountain Historical Western Romance Series

Description

His life is all about following the rules.
This obstinate cowgirl is all about breaking them.

Paradise Point, Book Eighteen, Redemption Mountain Historical Western Romance Series

Bram MacLaren is a man with a goal. Build a ranch in western Montana and expand the MacLaren name. Inking a partnership with the wealthy Pelletier brothers, there's nothing to stand in the way of the dedicated, hardworking rancher. Except the obnoxious and willful young woman intent on becoming the best wrangler in the western territory.

Selina Rinehart doesn't care about the odds. Becoming the equal of the men who run the horse breeding program at Redemption's Edge is what drives her. If others see her as cantankerous and selfish, well, so be it. Nothing will stop her from reaching her goal—except perhaps the Pelletiers' sanctimonious new partner.

Keeping their distance seems the best solution, until Dax asks Bram to takeover Selina's training.

The two butting heads amid their growing attraction isn't all that creates tension on the ranch. Someone's been abducting people off the streets of Splendor, as well as from a neighboring ranch. Adding to the danger, a series of earthquakes rocks the town and surrounding ranches, including Redemption's Edge.

Paradise Point, book eighteen in the Redemption Mountain historical western romance series, is a novel with an HEA and no cliffhanger.

Visit my website for a list of characters for each series.
http://www.shirleendavies.com/character-list.html

Paradise Point

Chapter One

Redemption's Edge Ranch
Splendor Montana
Spring 1872

Wild eyes glared down at the target sprawled on the ground, the intent clear in his mutinous glare. An eerie silence swept over the executioner and its prey, time slowing.

The sharp crack of a six-shooter from several yards to his side caught the killer's attention, giving the object of his rage a split second to roll away. Rising to his feet, he raced to safety.

Rearing back, two deadly hooves hovered over the spot where Bram MacLaren's head had been a moment earlier. A deep, throaty blow of agitation signaled the stallion's alarm at losing its prey. Hooves slamming to the ground, the horse snorted, circled, then dashed to the other end of the corral.

Rushing from the corral, Bram clamped a hand on his brother's shoulder. "Thanks, Thane. The beast was about to get the better of me."

"Seems you have more work to do, MacLaren." Selena, eyes bright with mirth, shot him a broad smile. "Want me to give him a go?"

"Nae." The hard, gruff response indicated his frustration with himself, and irritation with the young woman a few feet away. "You're no match for the devil horse, Selina."

Crossing her arms, the amusement fell away, replaced with steely resolve. "I can ride any horse you can. Probably better."

Bram studied her before turning away, tired of her sharp tongue. "Prickly lass," he muttered, brushing dirt from his pants. Dismissing her, his attention moved to the stallion staring at him from across the corral.

He'd bred and trained horses most of his life. Never had one challenged him as much as the chestnut beast.

Laughter drew Bram's attention toward his younger brother, Thane. At twenty-one, he'd grown into a handsome lad. Tall and muscled, his disarming smile charmed most lasses, including nineteen-year-old Selina Rinehart. At least it seemed so, until she punched Thane in the arm, spun, and marched to the barn.

"She's a tetchy one." Thane had moved beside him, his gaze still fixed on Selina. "I think she likes me."

An unexpected wave of jealousy gripped Bram. Unexpected and unwanted. He and the woman got along as well as a bear and porcupine. A tight grin tilted the corners of his mouth, thinking comparing her to a porcupine was unkind to the small, irritable animal.

"If you've an interest in the lass, you should make your attentions known."

A look of sheer terror appeared on Thane's face. "I'm not daft. She's too peevish for me. If I ever decide to settle down, it won't be with a woman as prickly as Selina."

Barking out a laugh, Bram clamped a hand on Thane's shoulder. "Aye, lad. That she is." He nodded at the stallion. "That horse will be easier to break."

"Not so far." Thane laughed as he walked to the gate, resting his hand on the latch. "You planning to try again?"

Raising his head to the sky, Bram estimated the time to be an hour from sunset. "Not today, lad."

He didn't have to explain further. They needed to return to their own ranch, check on their two ranch hands, and warm up the stew and biscuits leftover from the previous night.

Brothers Kev and Vince Lathan had been wanted for murder in Colorado when Bram and Thane arrived in Splendor during a Christmas blizzard. They'd also been hiding out in an abandoned ranch east of town. The same ranch the MacLarens now called home.

"I'll let Dax know we're heading out." Waving at Bull Mason, one of the Pelletier foremen and the husband of Selina's sister, Lydia, he took the porch steps two at a time. Lifting his hand to knock, he stepped back when the door flew open.

Selina rushed forward, almost running into him before stopping. Placing fisted hands on her hips, she glared at him. "Do you plan to move?"

Lips twitching, Bram worked to control a chuckle. "Beg your pardon, but I believe *you* almost slammed into *me*, lass."

Swiping a hand in the air, she huffed out an exasperated breath. "It doesn't matter. Would you mind standing aside so I may leave?"

Bowing, he stepped away, sweeping his hand in front of him. "I'll not be the one to stop you."

"Are you making fun of me?"

Straightening, his eyes twinkled with mirth. "Never."

A soft snarl left her lips before someone inside called his name. "Bram. Come inside."

When he looked back toward Selina, it was to see her hurrying down the porch steps.

"Thought I heard your voice." Dax Pelletier, one of the two owners of Redemption's Edge, followed Bram's gaze, spotting Selina. "That one is going to be trouble."

Glancing over his shoulder, a grin tugged at his lips. "Aye. The lass is a feisty one."

Motioning Bram to a chair in his study, Dax poured each of them a whiskey before sitting across from him. "Selina was ten when we rescued the orphans from a band of Crow Indians stalking them. She stayed quiet for a long time. The quiet stopped about the time she turned fourteen."

Bram leaned forward, resting his arms on his thighs, rolling the glass between his fingers. "Was there a reason?"

Dax chuckled. "She decided to become a wrangler. Selina's been training with Travis ever since." Scrubbing a hand over his stubbled jaw, he shook his head. "Her personality changed from shy to gruff and quarrelsome. Even her sister, Lydia, loses patience with her. As you've experienced, she'll take orders from Travis, but few others. You know Travis. He's not one to be ordering anyone around."

Bram nodded, thinking of the talented, taciturn man who ran the ranch's horse breeding and training operation. He and Thane had been working with him since striking the deal with the Pelletier brothers to help them expand the horse program. In the few months since arriving in Splendor, Dax and Luke had been able to double the number of contracts due to the MacLarens' participation.

"The lass is still young."

Dax pinned Bram with an incredulous look. "She'll be eighteen soon. Many women are married by that age."

Bram's lips thinned. The child in his mind didn't match with the fiery woman who'd targeted her anger at him a few minutes earlier. Thane had pointed out Selina wasn't a girl, but Bram had ignored his brother's taunts. Bram had done his best to hide what he considered an inappropriate interest in her, believing Thane would be a better match. Each time he saw her, the pinching sensation in his chest warned him he might be mistaken.

Frustrated with the direction of his thoughts, Bram tossed back the whiskey and stood. "Wanted to let you know Thane and I will be riding out."

Dax shoved up from his chair, walking to the door. "Any progress with the stallion?"

A grim smile broke across Bram's face. "Most stubborn horse I've ever come across. He'll be bending to my will soon."

"I'll be sure to watch. Selina believes she'll be the one to break him."

Bram's brows knit together. "Are you allowing the lass to work with him after Travis leaves for town, and Thane and I ride out?" Travis lived in town with his wife, Isabella. Unless weather prevented it, he rode home each evening.

Dax snorted, shaking his head. "No. And the ranch hands know not to allow her into the corral with any of the wild horses until you or Travis are with her. She's not happy about it, but I can't risk her life to fulfill one of our contracts."

Shaking Dax's outstretched hand, Bram looked around. Selina leaned against the outside wall of the barn, talking to one of the newer ranch hands. The young man sat on a bench, repairing a pile of rope. Turning back to Dax, he nodded toward them.

"Who's the lad?"

"One of five new hands we hired to help with spring roundup. He's the youngest at nineteen. Seems captivated with Selina."

Bram could understand. He shifted between wanting to strangle the young woman, and taking her into his arms.

"I wish the lad luck."

"So far, she's shown no interest in getting to know any man. Lydia thinks Selina sees them as competition."

Incredulous, Bram's mouth twisted. "Competition for what?"

A small grin lifted one corner of Dax's mouth. "If I knew that, I might figure the girl out. See you tomorrow."

Slowly taking the porch steps to the ground, Bram continued to watch Selina and the ranch hand. His jaw tightened at the interest shown by the young man, his chest squeezing when he heard the laughter coming from Selina. Laughter. He didn't believe she'd ever laughed around him.

"Bram!"

Forcing his attention away from the couple, he lifted a hand toward Thane. Their horses were saddled, the reins held in his brother's hand. Time to leave. Yet he hesitated. Bram knew why, and the reason irritated him. Telling himself he didn't care who Selina spoke with, he turned away. Jaw clenched, he closed the distance between him and Thane in a few steps.

Cocking his head, the younger MacLaren studied his brother. "Are you all right?"

"Aye." Untying the leather straps behind the saddle, he slipped on his jacket, knowing the temperature would drop quickly once the sun began to set. "Has Travis already left for town?"

Thane shook his head, still watching his older brother. "He's riding with us. Should be ready in a few minutes."

Cursing under his breath, Bram grabbed his horse's reins from Thane's hand. Without explanation, he walked toward to the hitching post outside the large barn.

"Did something happen with Dax?" Thane persisted.

"Nae. All is good." He wouldn't share their main topic of discussion was Selina. Nor would he mention Dax's comments about the cantankerous woman.

She reminded him of his sister, Heather, an expert rider and more than proficient with a six-shooter, rifle, or shotgun. She was now married. The contrary woman had ignored Caleb Stewart's efforts to court her, finally succumbing to the man who refused to give up on her.

Underneath, Bram knew Heather had a heart of gold, loved her family, and was devoted to Caleb. The couple ran a thriving cattle ranch in Settlers Valley, California.

Glancing over the top of his saddle toward Selina and the ranch hand, his eyes widened. The young man had finished his work repairing the pile of rope and stood. Leaning close, he whispered something in Selina's ear. Surprising Bram, she didn't back away. Instead, she threw her head back and laughed, then touched his arm.

Was she interested in the ranch hand? Being friendly? The last made him snort in disbelief. Friendly wasn't in Selina Rinehart's vocabulary.

"Got delayed."

Focused on the couple, Bram didn't notice Travis stopping beside him until he spoke.

"You two ready?"

"Aye, we are." Swinging into the saddle, Bram waited for Thane and Travis to do the same before riding away, not bothering to look back.

Chapter Two

Splendor, Montana Territory

Resting his back against the side of the jail, Enoch Weaver adjusted in the seat. His landmark black derby hat had been pulled low on his forehead, his eyes peaking from underneath.

Most would figure him to be what he appeared. A man sleeping off a large dose of whiskey from the night before. Their assumption would be quite wrong.

The truth about Enoch's true nature came to light when a gunman had tried to kill one of the deputies and his fiancée. The man many considered the town drunk, had saved both of them, while becoming a valuable resource to Sheriff Gabe Evans and his deputies.

Enoch had blossomed in the role of town watchdog, relaying information which might help avoid a shooting, burglary, or other disreputable deed. Gabe, his deputies, and the town leaders were the only ones who knew Enoch drew a small salary for sitting on one of the many benches around town, reporting what he saw.

Today was quiet. Not much had happened since the Christmas blizzard months before. It had been a night of the town coming together. A night few would ever forget.

Spring had rolled across the Montana plains earlier than normal, bringing with it warm weather. Melting snow had swelled the creeks, rivers, and lakes to overflowing.

The good weather had also brought an unusually large number of travelers heading west. A good number put down roots in and around Splendor. The newcomers were the ones who drew Enoch's interest. The bench rocking pulled his attention to the man who sat down beside him.

"See anything interesting?" Deputy Shane Banderas kept his gaze on the street, keeping his voice low.

Enoch gave a slow shake of his head. "New people, but nothing suspicious."

One corner of Shane's mouth quirked upward. "Bored?"

"I'm never bored, Deputy. People intrigue me."

"You must've been a good attorney." Shane's attention was drawn to two young couples on the other side of the street, for no reason other than how overdressed they were for a small, Montana town.

Enoch's heart tightened at the comment. Thinking of the past, the tragic deaths of his wife and son, often ended in several days and nights of drinking. It had been months since he'd let his thoughts wander in that direction.

"Those days are long in the past."

Shane understood. Many residents of Splendor came with haunted pasts, himself included. He nodded across the street. "Those four people been in town long?"

Enoch didn't turn his head, already knowing who Shane meant. "Came in on today's stage. By the looks of them, there's nothing for them here. They'll be gone tomorrow."

"Anyone else of interest?"

"Afraid not. Except for Old Will. Haven't seen him since well before Christmas."

Shane remembered the grizzled mountain man who'd lived in the mountains west of Splendor off and on for the last few years. Dax and Luke Pelletier kept watch for him from their ranch, occasionally sending men into the mountains to confirm the man's location. Most times, they found signs of Old Will's abandoned camps. Even their best trackers couldn't follow his trail.

"He traded furs at Petermann's store for food and such before heading out."

"Do you think it's true he lived with the Crow for several years?" Shane asked. The man had always intrigued him. The rumors were he'd left Virginia as a young man, working as a fur trader, Army scout, buffalo hunter, and wagon train guide.

"No reason to doubt it. The man speaks their language, and word is he travels through their territory without fear." Enoch shifted on the bench, clasping his hands together in his lap. "Old Will is more a ghost than a man."

Shane chuckled, understanding. Rumors surrounded the man who came and went, not showing up for months at a time. No one knew his exact age. Those betting guessed Old Will to be anywhere between forty and sixty. Standing, Shane glanced down at Enoch.

"I'll bring you some coffee."

Enoch waved him off. "Had my fill today. As soon as the sun sets, I'm heading back to my place. Let Gabe know all is quiet."

Shane clasped him on the shoulder. "Will do."

Sauntering off, the deputy scanned the street, stopping for an instant when he spotted the two couples. They'd crossed the street and now walked toward him. Something about one of the women seemed familiar.

Then it struck him. She was the exact image of a girl from his past. Angela Baldwin, a girl he'd once loved. A girl he'd been told had died at sixteen when a fever swept through their town.

Shaking his head, he whipped around to enter the jail. No sense torturing himself with memories of a beautiful girl who'd died much too young.

Gabe glanced up from his seat behind the only desk in the front office of the jail. He'd served as sheriff since not long after arriving once the war ended. His closest friend since childhood, Noah Brandt, already lived in Splendor, and encouraged him to stay.

"Shane."

"Gabe." Lowering himself into a chair, he stretched out his long legs, trying to clear his head of Angela's memory. "Enoch's on his way home. Said to tell you all is quiet."

Gabe set down the pen in his hand, leaning back in the chair. "It's been the same for months. My guess is Enoch's getting bored."

"I'm fine with quiet. In fact, I could live on quiet for quite a spell."

Chuckling, Gabe was about to respond when the door of the jail flew open. Deputy Hawke DeBell took a step inside. "Enoch collapsed on his way home. I took him to the clinic. Doc McCord is tending to him."

Standing, Gabe grabbed his hat. "Does Doc know what happened?"

"No. Maybe a heart attack. He'll know more in a bit. I'm heading back to the clinic." Hawke and Enoch had become close the last couple years. "I planned to walk him home. We went about a block before he collapsed on the boardwalk."

Gabe looked at Shane. "I'd appreciate it if you'd stay here. I shouldn't be long. Let's go, Hawke."

The streets were almost empty as the sun dropped behind the western range. The few people remaining waved to Gabe and Hawke, both nodded, but their thoughts were on Enoch as they hurried to the clinic.

Seconds before reaching the steps, the earth shifted under their feet. Grabbing a post, Gabe steadied himself, as did Hawke.

"What the..." Gabe's voice trailed off as the clinic, Ruby's Grand Palace, and other buildings swayed.

"An earthquake," Hawke responded at the same time the glass in one window of the clinic cracked.

Gabe's eyes widened. "Never been in one."

"I have. This is mild compared to the others."

Screams from down the street caught their attention when another tremor shook the ground.

"We need to help them." Gabe started to leave, stopping when Hawke grabbed his arm.

"Wait to see if there are more tremors. We can't help if we're injured getting to them."

"You're right. Let's check inside the clinic. I want to know how Enoch is doing. If anyone's been hurt, the town will need Doc's services." Gabe took the steps one at a time, ready in case the ground shook again.

Shoving the door open, he crossed the threshold, Hawke close behind him. Three examination rooms faced them, the door to one ajar, light from a lantern shining through the crack.

Striding across the open space, Gabe drew the door open. Before him, Enoch laid motionless on the bed, Doctor Clay McCord was bent down, checking the older man's breathing.

"How is he?"

Straightening, Clay's grim features met Gabe's worried expression. "He's alive. Breathing well, and his heartbeat is strong."

"Has he woken?"

"Not yet. It's probably best given the trauma to his body. Do you have any idea how old he is?" Clay walked around the bed, resting a hip against it.

Removing his hat, Gabe ran a hand through his hair. "Anywhere between forty and sixty."

"Fifty-two." The two men shifted to see Hawke leaning against the doorjamb. "Got it out of him before Christmas."

"And no family?" Clay asked.

"His wife and son were killed in an accident years ago. That's why he left Cincinnati and his law practice." Shoving away from the door, Hawke walked to the bed. "His color is a little better than when he collapsed."

Resting a hand on Enoch's shoulder, he startled when his friend shuddered under his touch. A choked moan brought Clay to the other side of the bed.

"Enoch, can you hear me?"

"You're shouting. Of course I can hear you."

Hawke covered his mouth to hide a grin while Gabe coughed and turned away.

"How do you feel?" Clay asked, checking Enoch's heartbeat and breathing.

"Fine." When he tried to sit up, he fell back on the bed and closed his eyes. "A little weak. What happened?"

"You collapsed."

Enoch's eyes popped open. "Collapsed?"

"We were walking to your cabin when you dropped to the ground," Hawke answered. "You didn't make a sound. I didn't have time to grab you."

Eyes closing again, Enoch fell silent for several long moments. Clay continued to examine him while Gabe and Hawke watched.

"There was no pain." Enoch focused on Clay, working hard to stay awake.

"Sometimes, there isn't."

Noise from the front had Gabe turning to the front room. Several people entered, most holding rags to their faces, arms, or chests.

Stan Petermann, owner of the general store and a town leader, approached Gabe. "We need the doc."

"Clay is with Enoch right now. Everyone have a seat and he'll see those with the most serious injuries first. I'll send Hawke to find Doc Worthington and round up the nurses."

"On my way." Hawke gave a brief wave before disappearing outside.

Gabe turned back to Stan. "Any more tremors?"

Touching a now soiled rag to the blood oozing from a cut on his cheek, Stan glanced toward the occupied examination room. "They stopped about ten minutes ago. Darn can fell off a shelf and hit my face."

Gabe could see the bruising on his friend's face. "Do you think there are others who were injured?"

"Besides the ones here? Don't know. I expect they'll be coming here if they're hurt."

"Hawke says it was an earthquake."

"He's right, Gabe. It's been a while since the last one. We were lucky then. The town was much smaller, and there were only a couple injuries. Scared the cattle, though. I imagine Dax, Luke, and the other ranchers are chasing strays right about now."

The front door flew open, Cash Coulter, one of Gabe's deputies, sauntered inside, a corner of his mouth lifting in a smirk. "Horace Clausen is trapped inside his bank."

Chapter Three

Bram and Thane hadn't spoken much during the trip back to their ranch. When they did, the men focused on the stallion, and how best to complete their work so they could move on to other horses. There'd been no mention of Selina, which suited Bram just fine. He'd been having a hard enough time getting the image of her and the young cowboy out of his head.

"Kev and Vince are doing the work of four men."

Thane's comment took Bram by surprise. "Aye, and we pay them well for their work."

"We could grow faster with more men."

"Takes money, lad."

Thane knew Bram didn't want to ask their Uncle Ewan for more funds. He and their Uncle Ian had provided them a large sum to expand the MacLaren horse operation into Montana.

It had been a surprise when the uncles approached Bram with their idea. They'd known he'd been ready to set out on his own for quite a while. His duty to the family, and their Circle M Ranch, kept him in California long after the time had come for him to make a change.

The uncles had known this. They'd waited patiently for Bram's ambition and their plans to expand the ranch to come together. Once Thane heard the news, he'd insisted on riding along. The only person hard to leave was their mother. Audrey had supported the decision, yet the brothers knew she'd mourn their leaving.

"Ewan and Ian will send us what is needed. They want this to succeed as much as us, maybe more."

Bram glanced over at him, lifting a brow. "No one wants this to do well more than me, lad."

Thane knew this was true. "We can't work long hours with the Pelletiers and build our own ranch without more men. Two more. Kev and Vince can watch over them, make certain they know what to do."

The two had the same conversation several times over the last few weeks. Bram had put off a decision, not ready to contact their uncles. After several long days at Redemption's Edge, he was ready to send the telegram.

Opening his mouth to respond, Bram's eyes narrowed when his buckskin gelding began dancing around. Thane's did the same, whirling in a circle before he reined in enough to control the animal. As the horses calmed, the brothers heard a deep rumbling sound coming from the ground.

"An earthquake," Bram barked. He didn't elaborate. Living in California, they'd experienced several earthquakes, some causing immense damage, others causing little.

Sliding to the ground, their grips tightened on the reins, preparing for more tremors. Until the ground calmed, they'd stay in place, reassuring their horses all would be well. After two more small tremors, then nothing for a period of time, they swung into their saddles.

"Didn't know they had earthquakes out here." Thane's voice held a hint of amusement. "Feels like home."

One corner of Bram's mouth turned up. "Aye, it does." Although, it really didn't.

Montana had colder winters, with snow and winds, which whipped through the thickest coat. The western region was vast, with peaks thousands of feet tall, predators not common back home, and Indians known to sweep into ranches to kidnap and steal. At the Pelletier ranch, everyone was on constant guard for a band of Crow who'd already tried to abduct Shining Star, a young Blackfoot woman...and new mother.

Right now, Bram refused to spend time considering the differences between Montana and California. Their ranch and possible damage filled his mind. He found himself sending up a brief prayer Kev and Vince were safe.

Cresting a small hill, they reined up, staring at the picture before them. It was as if the earthquake hadn't touched the ranch.

Kev and Vince worked together to break one of the mustangs they'd caught over the last few weeks. Nothing had changed since Bram and Thane left early that morning. Sharing confused looks, they quickly covered the distance to the corral.

Face red with humiliation, Horace Clausen brushed off his dark slacks and coat, mumbling under his breath.

Gabe, Cash, and a group of townsfolk gathered around. All solemn faced, waiting for him to speak.

"Are you all right, Horace?" Gabe's gaze moved over the man, seeing nothing except a frazzled banker.

"Fine, fine. What happened?"

"An earthquake." Gabe glanced behind him, noticing many in the crowd nodding in agreement.

"That's absurd. We don't have earthquakes in Montana."

An older man, tall, slender, with a gray mustache and beard, stepped forward. "Sure we do, Horace." Rubbing his jaw, he opened his mouth to say something else when one of the women spoke over him.

"It was about fifteen years ago. Don't think you were here when it happened, Horace. Wasn't as bad as the one today."

Horace shot a look at Gabe. "Were there injuries?"

"So far, nothing serious. Doc McCord is taking care of those who showed up at the clinic. Hawke's fetching Doc Worthington in case there are more."

"Our money safe, Horace?" This came from a short, scrawny man who looked as if he'd never saved a dime in his life.

"Of course it's safe, Marvin."

"Now that we know Horace, and your money, is safe inside the bank, you need to get back home. Stay inside the rest of the night, and don't use your lamps. Don't want them starting fires if there are more tremors."

"We won't be getting more, Sheriff." This came from the woman who'd experienced the quake fifteen years earlier. "They hit once and they're over."

"Don't believe that's always the case," Horace commented. "Even so, we're all hoping you're right."

"All right. Time to move on." Gabe let out relieved breath. He needed to get home, confirm his wife, Lena, and their children were all right.

"Sheriff, you got a minute?"

Resigned, Gabe turned his attention to Silas Jenks, longtime resident and owner of the lumber mill. "What can I do for you, Silas?"

"You know Amos Henderson returned a couple weeks ago." He mentioned the original owner of the Wild Rose, the saloon Gabe and his business partner, Nick Barnett, bought a few years earlier.

"Sure do. Had supper with him last week. I understand he may be staying."

Silas licked his lips, an odd expression crossing his face. "That's what he told me. The problem is, I can't find him."

A brow lifting, Gabe stared down at the shorter man. "Can't find him?"

"Not since last night. We had supper at the boardinghouse. He's staying there, you know."

Gabe nodded, anxious for Silas to get to the point.

"He asked me to meet him for breakfast this morning, but he didn't show. I went back at lunch. Suzanne said she hadn't seen him since supper last night. You know she doesn't come in for breakfast much anymore. Not with the baby." A small grin appeared on Silas's face. "When I asked, she talked to the cook and server who were there this morning. No one's seen him. I was on my way to the boardinghouse for supper, hoping I'd see him, then the earthquake hit."

Gabe found it curious, but wasn't concerned. People's plans changed all the time. A few years ago, Amos made a quick decision to sell the Wild Rose to him and Nick. He left town right afterward.

"Have you been back to the boardinghouse since the quake?"

"Just came from there. Amos hasn't shown up. Suzanne was busy cleaning up some glass that fell off shelves, but she looked upstairs. He wasn't in his room, but his clothes and such are still there."

"Maybe he decided to eat at McCall's or Eagle's Nest."

"I checked with Betts at McCall's. Amos hasn't been there for several days. He's not going to spend money at the Eagle's Nest. Too expensive for him. No offense, Gabe."

"None taken." As with the Wild Rose and Dixie saloons, he and Nick also owned the St. James Hotel and the Eagle's Nest restaurant. "I'll talk to my deputies, ask them to check around. They're dealing with a lot of scared people right now, but no reason they can't look for him while taking care of their other duties."

"That's great. I appreciate it, Sheriff."

"Doing my job, Silas. I'll send someone to the lumber mill or your house once Amos is found."

"You know I live above the mill."

Hiding a grin, Gabe gave a slight nod. "We all do, Silas. Now, I'd best get back to my duties and talk to the deputies."

Taking a detour by the clinic, Gabe checked on Enoch, glad to hear the older man was eager to go home. Doc McCord understood, but ignored Enoch's protestations.

Doing a quick sweep of the town, he explained about Amos to each deputy he encountered before stopping at the jail. His gaze landed on the desk, noticing a piece of paper. Reading it, he let out a relieved sigh. His father, Walter, had brought a note from Lena, letting him know they were all fine, the earthquake hadn't damaged their home, and they'd see him when he got home.

Folding the paper, he slipped it into his pocket, feeling his heart squeeze. He and Lena had been married five years, and he loved her more every day. Gabe couldn't imagine another woman who could ever fill his heart as much as his smart, beautiful wife.

The door opening behind him broke all thoughts of his family. He still had work to do before heading home. Turning, he saw Shane and Hawke, their expressions grim.

"No one has seen Amos since last night," Shane said. "One of the servers at the boardinghouse remembers him taking a walk after supper with Silas, but don't recall seeing him again."

Hawke lowered himself into a chair. "I spoke with Ruby at the Palace. He's been in a few times since coming back to town. The last time was two or three nights ago.

His horse is still at Noah's stable. He hasn't seen Amos for a few days."

Shane nodded. "Something's not right, Gabe."

"Silas is right to be worried," Hawke added.

Scrubbing a hand down his face, Gabe considered all that had happened in less than twenty-four hours. Enoch's heart attack, the earthquake, and Amos missing. The first two would work themselves out.

The last? Gabe had no idea what had happened to Amos Henderson. His mind sorted through various options, none optimistic.

"Gather up the rest of the deputies, including Beth. We're going to search for Amos, and we won't stop looking until he's found."

Chapter Four

Selina struggled to keep astride her mare when she reared back. Her wide eyes matched those of the horse. "Whoa, Honey." She stroked the mare's mane, all the while on alert.

She'd never experienced an earthquake, but didn't need to be told that's what shook the earth beneath them. Calming Honey, she slipped to the ground, talking in soothing tones to the mare she'd been given when becoming a part of the Pelletier family.

Her own breaths coming in gasps, Selina looked behind her at the trail leading to the ranch house. Bull Mason, one of the ranch foremen, and her brother-in-law, knew she'd left. He would already have at least one of his men looking for her.

A rush of regret passed through her. She knew it wasn't smart leaving the main ranch area minutes before the sun set. Bull had said as much. When he left to search for someone to accompany her, Selina had taken off.

"You've gotten yourself in a real mess this time," she muttered to herself, gauging the distance back to the ranch. As she did, another tremor shook the ground below her. Gripping the reins close to the mare's head, Honey danced around, but didn't rear back.

The sun had disappeared behind the western mountains, the sky now dark and foreboding. Selina didn't know what had prompted her to ride out alone. She winced at the lie. She knew exactly what, or rather who, provoked her to act in such a stupid manner.

"It's Bram MacLaren's fault." Everything bad, which had happened to her over the last few months, was caused by him. Holding the reins, she walked the trail back to the ranch, slowing occasionally to kick a rock or clod of dirt. "The man is an arrogant wretch. Don't you agree, Honey?"

As if she understood, the mare whinnied in answer.

A self-satisfied grin crossed her face before it vanished. "I'm as good a rider as him. Maybe better."

Stopping to mount her horse, she hesitated when the ground rumbled, rolling under her boots. Stroking Honey's neck, Selina's heart pounded. She'd heard stories of an earthquake long before she and the other orphans came to Redemption's Edge. The way the story was told, no one was injured, but as the intensity of the tremor increased, her concern for her family and the ranch increased.

Waiting until the tremblers subsided, she swung into the saddle. Covering the distance to the ranch, her thoughts centered on what she might find, praying there'd been no damage or injuries.

"Selina!"

The shout drew her attention. Relieved, she saw the newest ranch hand, Owen, riding toward her. Slowing, she allowed him to catch up.

"Bull sent me to find you. Are you all right?" His gaze moved over her, appearing to look for signs of injury.

"Fine. Is the ranch all right?"

"When I left, a few tools fell off their hooks in the barn, and some pots with flowers had turned over. No one was hurt. At least not that I knew about before leaving." Owen rode beside her, his gaze scanning the area as they continued toward the ranch. "Never experienced a quake before."

"Me neither. Hope I never do again."

The last mile continued in silence. Selina couldn't keep her thoughts from Bram. She'd heard Dax and Luke talk with Travis and Bull about the MacLaren ranch in California. The same as Redemption's Edge, Circle M was the largest in the northern part of the state, and equally successful. Dax and Travis considered Bram to be one of the best breeders and trainers in the western United States.

Selina had wanted to join the men, ask her own questions about Bram and Thane, but Rachel had called her to the kitchen. When she'd waylaid Dax later, he'd told her to ask Bram directly if she had questions. His surly, unapproachable manner squelched her curiosity.

When the ranch house came into sight, she let out a ragged breath. Even in the moonlight, it appeared the same as when she'd ridden out over an hour earlier.

Streams of smoke came from two chimneys, lanterns lit the interior, offering a welcoming glow. The closer they got, the more her heart rate slowed.

Reining to a stop, she slid to the ground, running up the steps and through the front door. Behind her, Owen watched, his chest squeezing. Grabbing Honey's reins, he rode to the barn, an odd sense of homesickness overwhelming him.

Splendor

"There's no trace of Amos." Shane lowered himself into a chair, tossing his hat on the desk. "No one's seen him since yesterday."

Gabe had made a quick trip to his house, confirming Lena, the children, and his father were fine. Eating a quick meal, he'd kissed his wife, riding back to the jail in total darkness. Shane was the third deputy to give him news he didn't want to hear.

"We have a three-quarter moon, but it's not enough to scour the area." Dutch McFarlin, a deputy who'd been with Gabe for several years, leaned against a wall, sipping a fresh cup of coffee. "We're going to need more than the deputies to mount an effective search."

Rubbing his temples, Gabe stared out of the front window as his mind sorted the possibilities. "His clothes are still at the boardinghouse, and his horse is at Noah's. Horace Clausen told Hawke all the money Amos deposited in the bank is still there. He was always real good about his commitments. Not meeting Silas for breakfast is a bad sign."

Shane steepled his fingers under his chin. "Who would've had a reason to take him?"

Gabe shook his head. "No one I know of. He's comfortable, but not rich. Everyone likes him, and he's the kind of man who'd give you the shirt off his back. Amos and Silas used to take turns playing Santa Clause each year for the children." He smiled at the thought before sobering. "We start the search at sunrise. Everyone should meet at the jail. Pass the word around. We'll take whatever help we can get."

Standing, Shane gave a mock salute before heading outside.

Finishing his coffee, Dutch set the empty cup on one of the shelves Noah had installed. Ever since Gabe had started ordering coffee for his hotels in New York, the jail had become a real popular place. Lena had purchased extra cups from Petermann's general store, and Josie Lucero and Olivia McCord's Emporium. Most of the deputies considered the ones from the Emporium too pretty for the jail, competing for the large, tin ones from the general store. As long as the coffee was good, Dutch didn't care.

"I want you to lead one group, Dutch. Shane will lead another, and Hawke a third. Cash, and Beau, Mack and Caleb, and Hex and Zeke will be tracking the area outside of town in groups of two."

"You know Beth won't be left out." Dutch mentioned Gabe's sister-in-law, Beth Cartman Evans. Married to Chan Evans, a U.S. Marshal, she'd become a deputy after a successful career as a federal agent.

"She's at the house with Lena and the children. Chan will join them when he returns from escorting a convicted prisoner to Deer Lodge. Until we know what happened to Amos, I'm going to leave her there. Depending on the results of the search, I may request Chan's help."

"He's a good tracker. Too bad he isn't here now." Dutch buttoned his coat, pulling the collar up as he walked to the door. "I'll help get the word out. See you at sunrise."

Gabe leaned back in his chair, mind whirling. He'd known Amos for years, since the first day he'd accepted the position as sheriff. The man didn't have an enemy. He worked hard, saved what he could, and helped others. The day Amos had left Splendor saddened a good number of people.

The longer he considered the disappearance, the more his unease grew. He recalled the kidnappers who'd traversed the country by train, identifying and killing random individuals. Their murderous spree ended in Splendor. Gabe didn't want to believe Amos's disappearance could be similar to what they'd faced in the past.

Scrubbing both hands over his face, Gabe shoved himself up. "You're creating a problem where one doesn't exist, Evans," he murmured under his breath.

Slipping into his coat, he stepped outside. He didn't intend to go home. Not yet.

One friend lay in the clinic, recovering from a heart attack. Enoch would be his first stop. Afterward, he'd make rounds, note damage from the earthquake. If time allowed, he'd go home, get a few hours sleep before meeting those searching for Amos.

He spent less than fifteen minutes in the clinic, watching Enoch sleep before closing the door behind him. Breathing in the cool night air, he walked along one street, then another, inspecting any damage he saw. There'd be more inside some of the buildings.

"Gabe."

Whirling around at the deep, strong voice, he recognized Griffen MacKenzie. He'd arrived last Christmas with Bram and Thane MacLaren. An attorney, he now partnered with Zeke Boudreaux's wife, Francesca, in her law practice.

Gabe accepted Griff's extended hand. "I heard Amos Henderson is missing. How can I help?"

Dropping his hand, Gabe's gaze traveled over the man. Over six feet tall and broad-shouldered, his pristine suit hid the ex-gunslinger underneath. From what Gabe knew, Griff could accomplish whatever he focused his keen mind on.

"Search parties are meeting at the jail at sunup. We'd appreciate your help."

Features solemn, Griff nodded. "Do you mind if I walk with you a bit?"

"Not at all. I'd appreciate the company. It's been a darn long day."

They walked in silence for several minutes before Griff spoke again. "Amos came to our office last week. Frannie asked if I would handle his request."

Gabe's brow rose. "Request?"

"He wanted to create a will. Seems his relatives care little about him. That's why he returned to Splendor." Griff stopped outside the meat market, studying a long crack in the front window. "Thought I'd left earthquakes behind when we left California. Anyway, I don't want to stir up trouble, but you might be interested in Amos's wishes."

"If you believe it might help us find him."

Lips twisting, Griff gave a mirthless chuckle. "Don't know about that, but it could help if he isn't found alive."

Halting, Gabe turned toward him, his expression unreadable. "What do you know?"

"Might be nothing."

"Any information could help, Griff."

Releasing a troubled sigh, he gave a sharp nod. "Seems Amos has a sizable estate. You know, he still owns his house at the edge of town"

"The one behind Silas's lumber mill?"

"Yes. Silas kept up repairs while Amos was gone. There's a married couple in there now. Rented it a few months ago. Both retired. According to Amos, they got tired of Omaha and headed west. Liked what they saw in Splendor, and decided to stay."

"That's the reason Amos is staying at the boardinghouse," Gabe muttered.

"Yes. He also owns property south of town. About five hundred acres. Not huge, but enough for a small cattle operation. He'd get a tidy sum if he wanted to sell it."

The information triggered a sick feeling in Gabe's gut. "Anything else?"

"Amos accumulated a large savings account over the years, adding to it when you and Nick bought the Wild Rose."

"How much?" Gabe asked. He released a slow whistle when Griff shared the total. "I had no idea."

"I'm guessing few people know about his wealth. From what I've learned, Amos lives a simple life. Nothing about him indicates *money*."

Gabe's gut twisted again. "What does this have to do with his disappearance?"

"The money doesn't. The beneficiary of his estate might."

A cold chill swept through Gabe, his throat constricting. Amos's estate was substantial. More than enough to spur a greedy person to take action if the money was needed.

"Who is it, Griff?"

Glancing around, his features hardened. "Silas Jenks."

Chapter Five

Bram stood on the stoop outside the kitchen's back door, sipping coffee while watching the sunrise. Puffy, white clouds dotted a crystalline blue sky, the same as the day before. Nothing to predict the earthquake of late yesterday. He wondered if today would be the same. A beautiful spring day ending with the earth churning below his feet.

Kev had been flying through the air when the tremors hit. Hitting the dirt, he stilled. The mustang he'd been breaking reared back, then danced around, nostrils flaring at the deep rumble from the ground.

Hustling out of the corral, he and Vince had held on to the top rail until the vibrations diminished. From what they'd told Bram and Thane, Vince had checked the barn for damage while Kev did the same inside the house.

By the time the MacLarens arrived, their ranch hands were back in the corral, acting as if nothing unusual occurred. A second search of the house and barn showed no damage.

Finishing his coffee, Bram tossed out the grounds before heading back inside. Thane, Kev, and Vince sat at the old kitchen table he'd bought from Noah Brandt. Their plates were full of eggs and ham slices.

"There's plenty, Bram." Thane continued to chew without looking up.

Grabbing a plate, he heaped the last of the food on it before joining the others. Taking a few bites, he broached the subject Thane had opened on their ride from the Pelletier ranch.

"What do you lads think about us hiring more ranch hands to help out?"

Neither spoke right away, although both stopped eating, their backs going rigid. Vince sent a solemn look at his brother, whose features were unreadable.

Bram sent them pointed glances. "Do you have an opinion?"

Letting out a breath, Kev answered. "It's your ranch, boss. Whatever you think is best."

Scooping up the last of his eggs, Bram chewed, studying the two young men. He knew Kev was nineteen, Vince eighteen. Unlike him and Thane, they had no family.

After their parents' deaths, the two had worked hard to save the family farm, which had been failing a little every year. The debt proved to be insurmountable. When the bank took over, the brothers packed their saddlebags and rode out, ending up at what they'd thought an abandoned ranch. The same ranch Bram and Thane purchased not long after arriving in Splendor. Over a short, few months, they'd become invaluable to the MacLarens.

Thane shifted in his seat, brows furrowed at the lack of response. "Don't you want some help?"

"We've been doing all right on our own, haven't we?" Kev's simple question had Bram rocking back in his chair.

"We've no complaints at all. The truth is, we can't expand with Thane and me working at the Pelletier ranch. It's too lucrative to walk away from the partnership. At the same time, you've proven your worth, lads." At the flicker in both men's eyes, a sense of understanding passed through Bram. "Your jobs aren't in jeopardy. Kev, we'd make you the foreman. We'd also expect both of you to talk to the lads we're thinking of hiring. I'm thinking two for now."

Visibly relaxing, Kev showed one of his infrequent smiles. "I'd be the foreman?"

Bram nodded. "Unless you don't think you're ready."

Brows shooting up, Kev's smile faded. "I'm more than ready."

"Vince, are you good with this decision?"

Head bobbing, the easy grin they'd come to expect transformed his previously grim face. "I think it's a real fine idea, boss. Kev will make a great foreman."

"Then we're finished here." Slapping both hands on the table, Bram pushed himself up. "Thane and I will stop in town on our way to the Pelletiers', and spread the word about us hiring."

The knowledge he'd soon be seeing Selina thickened his throat at the same time a grimace crossed his face. Why couldn't he have one day without the sour expressions and obstinate attitude of a woman bent on breaking the rules?

Confusion always accompanied any thoughts of the fiery cowgirl. A part of him couldn't stand being around her, while another craved her presence. He'd find his gaze searching for her while steeling himself for the verbal sparring inevitable when they were anywhere close to each other.

Slamming the back door behind him, he stomped to the barn, tacking up Bullet in record time. Aware of Thane's questioning gaze on him, Bram swung into the saddle, blowing out a resigned breath.

The amusement on Thane's face irked him. "Are you ready?"

"Whenever you are, Bram."

Heading out, Bram kept a brisk pace, letting the cool morning air strip thoughts of Selina from his mind. By noon, the temperature would rise to a point he'd be rolling up his sleeves, and mopping his brow.

Neither spoke until they entered the edge of town, reining up at the sight of men carrying rifles and shotguns. Everyone west of the Mississippi River carried a weapon. That wasn't a surprise. The stark expressions on their faces, intensity of their actions as they moved from one building to the next caught their attention.

"What's going on, Bram?"

"Don't know, lad, but I intend to find out."

Continuing to the jail, they nodded at Enoch Weaver, who sat outside with a blanket over his lap. It was a common sight to see the older man on the bench, his gaze wandering up and down the street. The blanket was new, as was the sallowness of his skin.

"No one's inside." Enoch hitched his thumb toward the jail.

"Where are they?" Thane watched one group of men standing outside the gunsmith shop.

"Gabe has everyone searching for Amos Henderson."

They waited for more, but when it didn't come, Bram asked the obvious. "Who's Henderson?"

"He used to own the Wild Rose. Sold it to Gabe and Nick Barnett right before he left town." Enoch coughed, rubbing his chest before continuing. "Came back a couple weeks ago, then disappeared sometime yesterday or the day before. According to those who knew him years ago, Amos isn't one to up and vanish." Releasing a heavy breath, he sagged into the bench, eyes closing.

Turning in a circle, Bram spotted Gabe across the street. "Thanks, Enoch."

The older man raised a hand before dropping it to his lap. Motioning to Thane, the two rushed toward the sheriff.

"Gabe. How can we help?"

Shaking their outstretched hands, he gave a short shake of his head. "Appreciate the offer, but I think we've got all the men we need." Removing his hat, Gabe scratched his head. "We've been searching for two hours and haven't found a trace of Amos. There are three groups in town and three pairs of deputies searching the perimeter of town."

Bram's lips pursed. "Two hours isn't much time, Gabe."

"I keep telling myself that, but it's already been almost thirty-six hours since anyone's seen him. His horse and clothes are where he left them. Hasn't taken meals at any of the restaurants. It's as if he turned into a ghost." Frustration tinged his voice. "Just about every able-bodied man is searching."

"Enoch said he's not one to disappear."

Gabe shifted to glance at the older man across the street. "He's right. Amos has no enemies, and is well liked."

He wouldn't mention the estate Griff disclosed. Gabe hadn't told anyone about it, not even his wife, Lena. He saw no sense creating additional questions around Amos's disappearance. Or generating suspicion toward Silas. Neither would benefit their search.

"If you're certain we're not needed, Thane and I will ride on to the Pelletier ranch."

"I'm certain. Did you have any damage from the quake?" Gabe added as an afterthought.

"We felt it, but no damage. How'd the town do?" Bram glanced up and down the street, seeing nothing obvious.

"Cracked windows, a few broken objects inside the buildings. Enough to scare a good number of the townsfolk. Had a couple tremors not long after the first one. Hope we're done with it."

"Sheriff, do you have a minute?" Silas rushed toward him, his face flushed. "Morning, Bram, Thane. You heard about Amos?" At their nods, he turned his attention back to Gabe. "Lewis at the newspaper thought of something you'll want to hear. He's finishing up today's paper or he would've come out with me."

"We'll be heading out, Gabe."

"Let Dax and Luke know about Amos. The men at Redemption's Edge used to spend time on Saturday nights at the Wild Rose before we bought him out. They'll want to know."

Redemption's Edge

Selina swept debris from the front porch, muttering to herself. She hated the chores Rachel gave her, preferring to work with Travis and the horses.

Head lifting, she searched the road from town. Bram and Thane were at least an hour later than usual. Selina didn't know why it mattered. The brothers set their own schedule with Dax, Luke, and Travis, and none seemed concerned. The fact she noticed their absence at all annoyed her.

"They don't belong here," she mumbled, the strokes of her broom becoming more forceful.

"What'd you say, Selina?"

Groaning, she straightened at Lydia's voice. "Nothing."

"Thought I heard you speaking with someone."

"Only myself." Holding the broom toward her sister, she shot a quick look toward town. Nothing. "Would you mind putting this away?"

Lydia offered a knowing glance. "I don't know why you fuss so much, Sel. Rachel relies on all of us to get the chores done."

Crossing her arms, she huffed out an exasperated breath. "But I work with the horses."

"Which is your choice. Your regular chores haven't changed. With Bram and Thane, Travis has more than enough help with the horses."

"Who says?"

"Dax."

Shoulders slumping, Selina dropped her arms to her sides. "He didn't say anything to me."

Walking to her, Lydia placed a hand on her sister's arm and squeezed. "It doesn't mean you can't help. Everyone here is proud of what you're accomplishing."

"Then why would Dax say that?" Lowering herself onto the porch swing, she clasped her hands together.

Sitting next to her, Lydia watched the play of emotions on her sister's face. "Probably because he counts the men *paid* to work the horses. You're more of an, well...an apprentice. Yes, that's it. You're in training with Travis and the MacLarens so you can someday earn a wage for what you do."

"I'm as good as Bram and Thane. Maybe better."

Lydia studied Selina's set features, her clenched jaw and pursed lips. They'd never lied to each other. Not when captured by the Crow tribe. Not since being rescued by the Pelletiers. She refused to start now.

"Do you want me to be honest?"

Shifting to face her, Selina gave an almost imperceptible nod.

Sighing, Lydia settled a hand over her sister's. "Although you're improving each day, your skills don't compare to the men's. I have no doubt, someday, you'll be their equal."

Swallowing the truth of Lydia's words, her mouth twisted. "But I'm not there."

A small smile lifted one corner of her mouth. "No...not yet."

Chapter Six

"Hold on, Bram." Thane guided his horse off the trail to Redemption's Edge toward what he thought to be a blanket thrown over a bush.

Normally, he wouldn't bother, not with them running late after their stop in town. Something about the fabric drew his attention. Drawing closer, he realized the blanket wasn't covering a rock, not unless the rock swayed back and forth, as this one did.

Sliding to the ground, Thane drew his six-shooter, approaching what he now believed to be a man. "Are you all right?" At no response, he asked again. This time, the man slowly turned before straightening.

Thane took a step backward at the man's appearance. Even bent over, the man had to be several inches over six feet, with broad shoulders. Beefy hands showed years of hard work. But it was the blood on his face that caught Thane's attention.

"You're bleeding." He made no move to get closer when the man's face twisted into a sneer.

"Darn right I am. Slipped off those rocks and landed on my face." Pulling a filthy handkerchief from a pocket, he mopped at the still damp blood. "You got any water?"

Grabbing his canteen, Thane handed it over.

Bram stood several feet away, listening to their conversation. He recognized the giant of a man. They'd met a month earlier in the Dixie saloon when Willem "Old

Will" Wright came down the mountain for supplies. Before making the long trek home, Old Will had downed three beers while watching a group of men play cards.

Stepping forward, he studied the gash on the man's face. "I'm Bram MacLaren. We met at the Dixie."

Old Will's hard gray eyes grazed over him. Turning mere inches, he spit out the blood in his mouth. "Don't recall." Lowering himself back onto the rock, he poured more water on the handkerchief, continuing to swipe at the blood.

Bram shrugged one shoulder. "Doesn't matter. We need to get you to the clinic in town."

"Ain't going to no doctor."

"The gash is deep. Probably needs sutures."

Those penetrating gray eyes glared back at Bram. "Don't need your help, and don't need a doctor."

Mouth quirking upward, Bram gave a terse nod. "Your decision, lad. Do you have a horse?"

"I ain't no lad."

Thane covered his mouth to hide a chuckle.

"My horse is a quarter mile back."

"I'll fetch him." Without waiting for a reply, Thane swung into the saddle and rode off.

Bram leaned a hip against a nearby rock, crossing his arms. "How'd you get this far from your horse?"

"Went after a deer. Missed the darn animal when I slipped off the rock." He motioned to the shotgun a couple feet away.

Brows furrowing, Bram tried to recall hearing a gunshot. "Didn't hear anything."

Old Will stilled before shaking his head. "Probably too far away. You coming from town?"

"Riding to the Pelletier ranch." Bram narrowed his gaze on the shotgun. Something about the story didn't make sense. Pushing away from the rock, he walked to the gun. Reaching out a hand, he glanced back at Old Will. "May I see it?"

His mouth twisted, but before he could respond, Thane joined them with Old Will's horse. Well, not a standard horse, but the scrawniest mule Bram had ever seen.

Fighting to keep his balance, Old Will stood, motioning for the mule. "Come here, Dolly."

The animal lifted her head, opened her mouth, but nothing except a strangled gurgle came out.

"She ain't got a voice." He stroked her neck. "Don't know what happened to her." He took the reins from Thane. "Come on, girl. We're wasting time." Without another word, the two followed the trail toward town.

Scratching his jaw, Thane watched them disappear. "Odd fellow."

"Aye, he is." Mounting Bullet, Bram reined him toward Redemption's Edge.

"You ever heard of a mute mule?"

Chuckling, he took one more look behind him before continuing on the trail. "Nae, lad, I haven't."

"You know what I think?"

Bram shot his brother a grin. "Nae, lad. What do you think?"

"I think Old Will got tired of the mule making those awful noises and cut out her tongue."

Bram thought the same, but decided not to share the information with Thane. It was a gruesome idea, and one he hoped was wrong.

Enoch had talked about Old Will one afternoon when Bram shared a flask of whiskey with him. He'd said the mountain man relocated his camp all the time. Searches for him turned up nothing, and no one had ever heard the braying of his mule. It had to make a person wonder.

Rounding the last turn in the trail, the Pelletier ranch house and barn came into view. The couple hundred yards separating them didn't impair the view to the woman working with one of the mustangs.

Selina. The cantankerous woman who got his heart racing with the smallest of smiles before ruining his mood when she opened her mouth. He'd never known a more tetchy female.

Bram saw the moment Selina spotted them. Instead of returning his wave, she whirled around, disappearing into the barn. The snub no longer angered him as it had when he and Thane first took the job with the Pelletiers.

He had no time for a petulant woman. They were late, and the Army required five more horses to fulfill their contract. The small herd was to be delivered to Fort Connall in a week. Four men could make the trip in a short two days. Bram wanted to get the contract completed so they could focus on the larger contract for Fort Laramie in Wyoming.

Taking care of their horses, they grabbed halters and coiled ropes before meeting Travis in the corral closest to the barn. As Bram suspected, Selina stood on the lower rung of the fence, arms resting on the top rail. Travis worked a mare in the center.

Not signaling their approach, Bram stopped a few feet away from her while Thane took a position by the gate.

"You're late." She didn't look at him when the words hissed out.

"Not your concern, lass."

Mouth twisting into a grimace, she turned toward him. "You work for the Pelletiers, which makes it my concern."

Bram couldn't hide the amused glint in his eyes. "Seems there's one way to work it out. We'll speak with Dax."

Jaw tight, the color leached from her face. Selina knew Dax, and his brother, Luke, would side with Bram. The MacLarens had their own ranch to run, and were working for the Pelletiers as much as possible. Selina knew she'd look foolish if Dax knew what had been said. She didn't let go of her grip on the top rail.

"He's too busy to be interrupted."

"Ah, giving up so soon, lass?"

Jumping to the ground, she stepped to within two feet of him. "I've asked you to stop calling me that."

Crossing his arms, Bram leaned against the fence, a knowing smirk on his face. "You have two choices. Lass or lad. I'm fine no matter which you choose."

It had taken her forty-eight hours after the MacLarens first arrived at the ranch in February to demand he not call her lass. There'd been no reason for the ultimatum. He and Thane had been standing with Dax and Luke when she'd made the pronouncement. The instant she whirled to walk away, all four men had chuckled. Months later, the memory still amused him.

Instead of answering, Selina's attention shifted to Rachel, who stood on the front porch, calling her name. Bram was certain her shoulders slumped.

"I'm needed in the house." Wincing for sharing the justification for leaving, she hurried off.

Lips twitching, Bram watched as she spoke with Rachel, Selina's arms flaying, emphasizing whatever she said. Rachel stood with her arms crossed, saying nothing as Selina presented her case. He had no doubt she argued to forego chores around the house in favor of working with the horses. From the expression on Rachel's face, the younger woman was failing.

"Do you want to work with the stallion, or should I give him a try?" Thane stood next to him, his gaze moving from Bram to the drama unfolding on the porch. "What's going on?"

"I'm guessing the lass is trying to get out of her chores."

Chuckling, Thane shook his head. "She's never succeeded before."

"The lass doesn't learn lessons well." Turning away, he saw Travis approach the stallion, a lead strap and halter in his hand. "You stay by the gate."

Entering the corral, his movements were restrained, cautious in the way he moved toward a wild animal. They'd spent a total of two days trying to break the stallion with little progress. Their time was short. Within days, they'd be leaving for Fort Connall, with or without the obstinate animal.

The contract specified the inclusion of one stallion, an odd request. Most agreements were fulfilled with geldings and the occasional mare. Colonel Miles McArthur had been specific. He wanted a stallion, and Dax had agreed to the terms.

Bram could hear Travis talking in a low voice, doing his best to calm the feral beast. Most horses took to the longtime wrangler in a short period of time. He'd been born with a gift unlike anything Bram had ever witnessed.

In an action smooth and quick, Travis slid the harness over the horse's head. Rearing back, the stallion attempted to break away. Travis's fast response and strong hold on the lead strap kept the animal under control. As much control as possible with the over one thousand pound beast.

Keeping his distance, Bram stayed alert, moving as Travis shifted his stance. It would take a mere second for the stallion to take control, rear back, and land a killing blow.

"You have him, lad." Bram knew Travis didn't need his encouragement. He also understood it didn't hurt when breaking a horse.

Several minutes later, the stallion stilled, ears pressed against its head. The three men knew within a few seconds, a minute at most, he'd rear back again. Travis never stopped talking, scooting close enough to run a hand down the animal's nose. Getting no response, Travis repeated the motion, glancing at Bram with a raised brow.

"Get the saddle."

Bram nodded, motioning for Thane to grab the saddle. Keeping his gaze trained on the horse, he handed it to Bram, who waited for Travis's signal. It wasn't long in coming.

A quick flick of his wrist had Bram walking forward. Unlike their other attempts when the horse snorted, danced around, and reared up on his back legs, this time, he remained calm. The odd behavior had all three men on alert.

Minutes passed, no one moving, watching the stallion's wide eyes study each of them. His ears had released, standing straight into the air.

Catching Bram's attention, Travis gave an almost imperceptible nod of his head. Inching forward, Bram stopped within a foot of the stallion, and waited.

When nothing happened, Travis tightened his hold on the lead strap and signaled again. Bram didn't hesitate.

Settling the saddle over the animal's back, he grabbed the cinch, tightening it around the horse's girth before mounting. One...two...three seconds passed before the stallion reacted to the intrusion. A series of short, forceful snorts were the only warning Bram had before the horse reared back and bucked.

Gripping the saddlehorn, Bram held on, vaguely aware of the shouts coming from Thane. He refused to be bucked off this time. Today, he would ride this horse.

Chapter Seven

Selina dried the last pan, muttering to herself. She hated cooking, and cleaning up even more. Yet Rachel, her sister, Lydia, and Luke's wife, Ginny, were determined to prepare her for life as a rancher's wife. Selina had lost count of the number of times she'd insisted marriage wasn't for her.

Sewing, cooking, planning meals held no appeal. She wanted to work with horses, someday be as good as Travis...or even Bram. Although the last would never be voiced. The brash Scotsman could never know how much she admired him. She shuddered to think how much more arrogant he'd be if he ever knew.

Shouts and whistles had her rushing to the front window. Staring toward the corral, her eyes widened. A group of ranch hands hung onto the fence, whooping and hollering as Bram rode the stallion. She'd seen him tame many horses, but the sight of him today had her breath catching.

Setting down the pan, Selina rushed out the front door to the corral. Bram was magnificent. Holding the saddlehorn with both hands, his total focus stayed on the horse. The relentless bucking didn't deter Bram, not even when the stallion came within inches of the fence.

One leg slammed against the rails, but didn't dislodge Bram before the animal bucked toward the center of the corral. Dancing in a circle, the sharp blowing sounds slowed. The horse raised and lowered his head several times, the snorts dissolving into a resigned whinny.

The people around the corral quieted, everyone waiting for the stallion's next move. Instead of exploding into action as they expected, the horse snorted several more times, giving up the fight.

Approaching from the front, Travis spoke in soothing tones, stroked the animal's neck, then slid the bridle into place. Giving the stallion time to adjust, he handed the reins to Bram and stepped away.

Selina held her breath, waiting to see if the horse would yield to Bram. The stallion moved forward after a soft roll of his rider's heel. Shaking his head, he continued to walk. First, straight ahead, then in a wide circle in response to Bram's signal.

"He's done it."

She glanced beside her to see Thane a foot way. "Yes, he has. I suppose you'll work with the other horses now."

A grin tipped the corners of Thane's mouth. "We've almost fulfilled the contract. The last few won't be as difficult as the beast in the corral."

Narrowing her gaze on the younger MacLaren, she turned to face him. "How do you know?"

"They were part of the stallion's herd. They're used to taking direction from him, and more docile. Once they see Bram riding him, the others will surrender."

"If that's the reason, why didn't you work on the stallion from the beginning?"

"The first mustangs came from a different herd. Bram broke their stallion early," Thane answered, his attention riveted on his brother.

"The horse Dax and Luke gave you for your ranch." Disdain was clear in her voice. She'd disagreed in the decision to let the MacLarens claim the stallion.

"It was part of our agreement with the Pelletiers. We were allowed one stallion." Thane thought of the majestic horse now secured in a corral back at their ranch. His lines and disposition would benefit their breeding program. "Colonel McArthur is going to have his hands full with that one." He nodded toward the horse Bram led around the edge of the corral.

Snorting, she stepped up on the bottom rail of the fence, resting her arms on top. "He looks docile to me."

Seconds passed before the stallion reared up, bucking several times while Bram brought him under control. Heat rose up her cheeks. Selina hated being proved wrong.

"He has a temper on him. Dax told us McArthur is a good horseman. Hope he's right." Thane left her to meet Travis at the gate. "Which horse is next?"

A rare grin appeared on Travis's face. "The chestnut mare. After the stallion, she shouldn't be too difficult. Do you want to break her?"

Excitement rushed through him. "I'll get her ready."

Luke Pelletier stepped away from the group of ranch hands. "All right. The excitement is over. Get back to your work." Glancing into the corral, he joined Travis. "McArthur will be satisfied with him."

"But can he handle the stallion?"

"Doesn't matter to us. He'll pay what we agreed. The rest is up to him." Luke's attention fastened on Bram, who rode the stallion toward the gate. "Where will you keep him?"

"The large stall. It won't take more than two days to complete the work. We'll leave for Fort Connall soon afterward." Grabbing two ropes, Travis released the gate, holding it open for Bram to pass through. Handing one rope to Luke, they waited.

Expecting the stallion to attempt escape, the men's attention didn't waver from horse and rider. If he did rear back, they'd be ready to toss ropes over his neck. It was a move both Travis and Luke had done a hundred times before.

As before, the ranch hands stopped their work to watch. Few had seen such a magnificent animal brought to heel. Bull Mason picked up a rope, loping toward them, slowing as he reached Luke.

The three spread out, ready to throw loops over the stallion's neck if anything spooked him. A frightened horse could do great damage in a short period of time. They refused to let that happen.

Surprising everyone, Bram guided the docile horse to the outside of the barn and dismounted. Sweeping a hand along his neck, he whispered words of encouragement. When nothing happened, he led the animal into the largest stall, removed the saddle and bridle, and closed the door behind him.

"I'll be," Bull said, removing his hat to shred fingers through his hair. "Never seen such an ornery horse give up so easily."

Luke clasped his friend's shoulder. "Nothing easy about that horse, Bull. He may be planning his next attack while we're watching."

Chuckling, Bram looked into the stall, confirming the amount of hay. "What should we name this beast, Travis?"

"I believe you already did, Bram. *Beast* fits him."

Selina leaned against a post in the barn, arms crossed. She loved the smell of wood, straw, and leather, and enjoyed listening to the banter between the men. Travis was right. *Beast* fit the stallion. She didn't believe the horse had given up hope for escape.

Shouting drew her attention. Shoving away from the post, Selina walked outside to see Bull standing in the center of the corral. The mare already wore a bridle and saddle, the reins in his hand. Thane stood beside the horse, running a hand along her neck, shoulder, and withers. Like Bram and Travis, he spoke in a soft voice. As he did, the animal's ears released from being pinned against her head.

Nodding at Bull, he took the reins from the foreman's hand. In a swift move, he swung into the saddle, waiting for the mare's reaction. A loud whinny broke the silence an instant before she launched herself into the air.

Thane held the reins while tightening both hands on the saddlehorn, holding on, hoping the horse would buck herself into exhaustion. Moving across the corral, she showed surprising endurance. Whirling around, the mare headed in the opposite direction, her energy fading.

Blowing out a last, forceful snort, the mare stopped beside the fence. Her wide, frightened eyes searched for an escape, body vibrating with the need to run away.

When Thane believed she'd calmed enough to make a turn of the corral, she began to dance. That's when he heard the slight roar, saw the men disperse.

"Earthquake," Bull said. "Slide off and let the mare run, Thane."

He did as the longtime foreman said, watching the horse rush to the other end of the corral. Feeling the ground below him shift, Thane tore his gaze away from the mare. The same as Bull, he reached out, grabbing the fence to steady himself.

"Guess we aren't free of the quakes yet." Bull shot a look around, seeing Selina join Lydia and Rachel on the porch. Thane understood Bull's concern about his family.

"All the children are probably inside. The women aren't going to let anything happen to them," Thane assured him.

The shaking grew stronger as the words left his mouth. The groaning sounds of wood against wood drew their attention to the barn. A moment later, a loud crash came from inside, dirt and straw flying into the air.

Muttering a curse, Bull made his way to the barn, arms outstretched for balance, followed by Selina. Tripping when a small fissure broke the ground, landing him on his knees. Thane reached out a hand, helping him up as Travis stumbled out of the barn, followed by Bram, his arm around Selina. Choking, they fell to the ground, swiping at their eyes.

A loud creaking noise sounded an instant before the porch roof shuddered, tearing away from the house. Screams and shouts came from inside.

"They may be hurt." Selina pushed up on shaky legs, moving toward the house.

"Selina, wait!" Bram tried to stop her, tripping twice before gripping her arm at the same time the porch stairs shifted, one side collapsing. "Stay here. I'll check on those inside."

Her eyes gleamed with determination. "I'm going with you."

Travis took hold of her other arm, pulling her against him. "Bram, Bull, and Thane will go inside. You'll be staying here. It's safer out in the open."

"They're my family. You can't keep me here."

Travis glared down at her. "I sure can. Now, stop struggling while the men search the house."

She huffed out her frustration, but stopped trying to pull from his grip. Her gaze fixed on the three, who avoided the stairs by jumping onto the porch. The ground had stopped shaking. Still, the men took deliberate steps, steadying themselves on the side of the house before shoving the door open.

Unable to stay outside a moment longer, Selina tugged free of Travis's grip and ran to the house. The devastation stopped her for a moment, until hearing shouts from the men.

Bull took the lead, yelling for Lydia and Joshua, their young son. He continued shouting their names while Bram and Thane searched for the others.

"Papa!" A door in the downstairs hall opened, wide eyes landing on Bull. Running to him, Josh jumped into his father's open arms. "Mama bumped her head, and Aunt Rachel hurt her arm, and Aunt Ginny fell down."

"Where is Mama?" Bull tightened his arms around his son, his voice shaking with emotion.

Twisting, Josh pointed down the hall. "There, Papa."

He closed the distance in seconds, pushing the door open. Lydia sat on the bed, dazed from a large knot on her head. A small rivulet of blood streamed from the wound, flowing past her left eye and down her cheek.

Setting Josh down, Bull knelt in front of Lydia. Bruising had already started. Removing a handkerchief, he dabbed at the blood. "Sweetheart, can you hear me?"

Dull, hazel eyes opened to meet his gaze. "Bull?"

"I'm here." Lifting a hand, he brushed hair from her forehead. Glancing over his shoulder, he expected to see Rachel and Ginny. "Where are the others?"

"Whaaat?" She touched the bump on her head, wincing.

"Josh said Rachel hurt her arm and Ginny fell down, injuring her hip. Do you know where they are?"

"I think Dax and Luke took them to the kitchen."

Josh slid his small hand into his mother's. "Mama, are you hurt?"

Looking down at her son, she forced a tight grin. "Mama's fine, Josh."

"I need to get you a cool compress." Standing, he swept Lydia into his arms. "Come on, Josh."

"Bull, put me down."

"No." Stepping over the threshold, he came to an abrupt stop. "What the…"

The windows and back door were broken beyond repair. Dishes, pots, and pans were strewn across the floor, as were ruptured bags of flour, sugar, and beans.

What he didn't see was any sign of the Pelletiers…or Thane.

Chapter Eight

Splendor

"Did you feel that, Gabe?" Shane stayed in place on the boardwalk, senses on alert. They'd just left the boardinghouse restaurant, completing their search for Amos Henderson before heading for the jail.

"No. What was it?"

Shane glanced up and down the street, seeing nothing amiss. The riders, wagon driver, and those walking continued as if nothing had happened.

Grimacing, he gave a tight shake of his head. "Thought I felt the ground rumble. Must've been my imagination."

Crossing the street, Gabe's gaze landed on Enoch. As had become the custom, the older man sat on the bench outside the jail, hands clasped in his lap, hat pulled low. The posture was part ruse, part a way for Enoch to feel as if he belonged.

Gabe and his deputies knew the man's story, understood his need to stay distant from others without shunning everyone. As he rested on the bench, he kept his gaze moving. More than once, he'd alerted Gabe, or one of his deputies, of pending danger.

"Enoch." Gabe sat next to him, stretching out his legs, while Shane lounged against a post. "How are you feeling?"

"Wish people would stop asking," he groused, eliciting grins from the other men.

"You put a scare into us. Don't want to lose my most effective master spy." Gabe watched a group of cowboys he didn't recognize ride past.

Lifting his head, Enoch snorted, lips twisting into a wry grin. "Master spy, am I?"

"Best I have." Seeing the cowboys stop outside the Wild Rose, Gabe drew in his legs, preparing to stand.

"I'll go," Shane said. "See you later, Enoch."

"That would be Master Spy to you, young man."

A grin tugged at the corners of Shane's mouth. He liked the older man. They all did. The heart attack had troubled everyone. Enoch had become an integral part of their lives, important as a friend and the town snoop.

Tipping his hat at three women he walked past, Shane's gaze narrowed on the cowboys who entered the Wild Rose. It was unusual to see a large group and not recognize a single one. He hadn't heard anything about the Pelletiers hiring, and they were one of few ranches big enough to take on more than a couple ranch hands at a time.

Pushing the swinging door, Shane crossed the threshold, noting the men at a table in a corner. A barmaid approached them with a tray of drinks. One reached out, sliding his hand around her waist. When his hand went lower, the woman deftly stepped away, keeping her distance as she handed drinks to the other cowboys.

Sliding into an empty spot at the bar, Shane accepted a whiskey from the bartender. His gaze went to the large mirror. Sipping, he watched the table in the large mirror behind the bar.

Finishing their drinks, one raised his hand to order another round. They joked and laughed. Their voices never rose, nor did they become boisterous or obnoxious.

Waiting until one of them dealt cards from the pack in his pocket, Shane tossed back the whiskey he'd been nursing. They'd given him no reason to stay, and he still had rounds to make. Pocketing the coin the bartender refused to accept, he stepped onto the boardwalk.

Stretching his arms above his head, Shane swiveled from one side to the other. He planned a much needed night's sleep before meeting another group of men at sunup. A group of men, who refused to give up the search for Amos, would be meeting for a second morning at the jail.

Gabe had designated three other deputies to join them. Shane had no idea where else to search. They'd scoured the town and surrounding areas for eight hours today without success. He doubted tomorrow would be different.

"Deputy!"

Turning at the shout, his stomach twisted at the sight running toward him. Shane swore it had been his imagination when he'd seen her with three others a few days ago. The closer she got, any doubt fled.

Angie Baldwin, the woman he'd once loved. The girl who'd died at eighteen, or so he was told, ran toward him.

Closing his eyes, he shook his head. Eyes popping open, he expected the vision to be different. It wasn't.

"Deputy. You must help me. My fiancé…" Her voice faltered as she raised her head to meet his gaze. "My…um…fiancé…" Blinking, a hand went to her throat as color drained from her face.

Reaching out a hand, he steadied her, his heart pounding. "Are you all right?" When she began to sway, he gripped her arm, leading her to a nearby bench. "Sit down a minute, then we'll talk about your fiancé."

Rushing to the saloon door, he motioned to a barmaid. "Bring me a clean, damp cloth." Seconds later, she handed it to him. Pressing it to Angie's forehead, he dabbed her cheeks, relaxing when the color returned.

Taking several slow breaths, her gaze locked on his once more. Lifting a hand, she touched his jaw, staring into bright green eyes she'd once known so well, before dropping her arm.

"You must think I'm simple, but you look so much like someone I used to know." Her voice wavered, but she didn't move her gaze from his.

Several seconds passed before he licked his lips. "It's me, Angie."

Eyes wide, she clasped her chest. "What?"

"It's Shane. They told me you were dead."

"Selina, can you hear me?" Bram knelt on the ground at the back of the house, his gaze focusing on an angry gash to her head. Beside him, Dax tended to Rachel's arm, and Luke took care of the injury to Ginny's hip.

When the last vibration hit, the men had carried their wives out of the bedroom, shouting for Lydia and Josh to follow. Selina had led the group, rushing through the kitchen's back door, not noting the stoop had collapsed until too late.

The others could do nothing when she'd lost her balance, falling to the ground. Rachel and Ginny had insisted they could get down on their own. No matter how they'd tried, neither had made it without the help of their men.

"Selina, lass. Can you hear me?" Pressing a cloth against her injury, his brows furrowed in growing concern. It took little time for it to soak through.

"Here." Thane handed him a bucket with a small amount of water, and a second clean cloth. "That's quite a wound. Has she opened her eyes?"

"Nae."

Dax knelt beside Bram, brows knit in concern. "How is she?"

"The lass hasn't woken." As the words left his mouth, her eyes popped open. Recognizing him, she squirmed, batting at his hand.

"What are you doing? Get away from me." When she attempted to sit up, he pushed her back down. "Stop it." She swatted at him again, which Bram ignored.

"You've been hurt. Stay put until the bleeding stops."

Lifting her hand, Selina touched her head, wincing. Blinking several times, she looked past Bram to the missing steps.

"I fell."

"Aye. Right on your head. Doubt it will cause much damage, lass." Rinsing the cloth, he pressed it once more to the gash, ignoring her huff of anger.

"Why is that?"

Meeting her gaze, a grin twisted his mouth. "You're the most hardheaded lass I've ever known."

Before she had time to respond, Dax touched her shoulder. "You scared us, Selina. How do you feel?"

"I'd be better if you'd help me to sit up." Taking her proffered hand, Dax tugged, his other hand supporting her back.

Bram stood, wiping his hands down his pants before a movement yards away caught his attention. Billy Zales rushed toward him, his expression grim.

"I can't find Shining Star or the baby," Billy choked out. "They were outside in the garden when the quake hit. I've looked everywhere."

Shifting, he motioned for Thane to join them. When Dax moved to stand, Bram held up a hand, stilling his movement. "We'll search for Shining Star while you tend to the lasses."

The three ran toward the large garden the Pelletier women tended every year. "Where was she the last time you saw her?"

Billy pointed to the empty basket. "Shining Star uses that to carry her tools. She would never leave it behind."

"Unless she and the baby were in danger." Thane turned in a circle, seeing nothing to help in the search. "Where have you looked for them?"

"I made a quick circle of the house and back in those woods." Billy indicated a patch of shrubs a few yards away. "She knows not to wander off without letting me know."

Bram and Thane knew the story. Shining Star had been brought to the Pelletier ranch by her Blackfoot grandfather, Running Bear, and her brother, after a Crow brave had dragged her into the forest, taking her maidenhood. When the pregnancy became obvious, the Crow had returned three times, trying to steal her away. To save her, Running Bear took her to the one place the brave wouldn't find her.

Billy had been ordered to stay with Shining Star, keep her safe. The baby boy had been born not long after Christmas. Over those months, the two had become close, although Billy had yet to voice his love for the beautiful Blackfoot woman.

Billy ran a hand through his hair before slamming his hat back onto his head. "We have to find her."

"We will, lad. I'm guessing the lass took her bairn and ran into the woods when the earthquake started. She's probably scared, waiting for you to find her." Bram studied the area where Shining Star had last been, spotting moccasin tracks in the dirt. They appeared to be going to the left. Billy stood beside him, seeing the same as Bram.

Swallowing the agonizing lump in his throat, Billy's mouth drew into a tight line. "We should split up. I'll go left." He didn't wait for the others to respond.

Bram motioned for Thane to search the area to their right. "I'll take the area in between. Billy! Two shots in the air will signal one of us has found them."

Waiting until the two had disappeared into the bushes, Bram took a quick look behind him. Relief rushed through him seeing Rachel and Ginny standing in the open kitchen door. Outside, Dax and Luke lifted Selina into the house.

It was time to find Shining Star.

Chapter Nine

Splendor

Angie's chest heaved, breaths coming in gasps. Shane Banderas, the boy she'd loved with all her heart, stood before her. A boy no longer.

"Shane?" Her voice shook on the question, brows drawing together in disbelief.

Instead of answering, his jaw tightened. Gripping her arm, Shane pulled her from the bench. "We'll speak in the jail."

Allowing him to draw her down the street, she studied the man who was so similar to the boy, yet much different. She'd been ten, him fourteen, when they'd met at church. Even at her young age, Angie had known Shane Banderas would be an important part of her future. He'd thought her a nuisance, sparing her nary a glance.

Time had passed, she'd become a young woman while he'd grown into a strapping man. At seventeen, Shane had shown up at her home. Following a long, private discussion, her father had given his consent for Shane to court her. Months later, he'd asked permission to marry her. Accepting his proposal had been the happiest day of her life.

A few days later, Shane disappeared, taking with him her future, and all their dreams.

The sound of a door scraping against an uneven, wood floor ended her reminiscing. She stiffened when Shane motioned to a chair across the desk from a large man with hard, piercing eyes.

"Sheriff, this is Angela Baldwin. She's saying her fiancé," he glanced down at her before continuing, "is missing. I brought her straight here."

"It's a pleasure, Miss Baldwin. I'm Sheriff Gabe Evans. What's your fiancé's name?"

Hands clutching in her lap, she forced herself to concentrate on the sheriff in front of her, and not the man looming over her. A blanket of cold wrapped around her, crushing her chest. If only their friends hadn't decided to travel on to San Francisco the day after arriving.

"Miss Baldwin? I'll need your fiancé's name."

"Carson Bartholomew Winslow."

Gabe tapped his pen on a piece of paper. "What brought you to Splendor?"

"We were traveling to San Francisco with friends of ours. They traveled on the day after we arrived. Carson wanted to stay on a few days."

"Without a chaperone?" Incredulous, Shane shifted to lean against a corner of the desk.

"Well...yes. We knew it wasn't quite appropriate, but we have separate rooms on different floors of the St. James."

Gabe shot a cautionary look at Shane. "Why do you believe Mr. Winslow is missing?"

"Carson failed to meet me for breakfast or lunch. Neither time did he leave a message for me. That isn't like him, Sheriff. He's always punctual. Carson would never cause me worry."

Jotting down notes, Gabe let out a breath. "Did you have someone at the hotel check his room?"

"Yes. Thomas opened his room. Carson's clothes, satchel, and a pair of boots are still there. So is the book he brought with him." Leaning forward, her hands grasped the edge of the desk. "He's gone, Sheriff. Carson would never have left me voluntarily."

Casting a glance at Shane, Gabe stood. "Let's go to the hotel. I want to check his room and speak with Thomas and any other members of the staff who may have spoken with your fiancé. Shane, you'll be coming with us."

"But—" Gabe's hard glare stopped Shane's argument. Nodding, he held out a hand, assisting Angela from the chair.

Stepping outside, she looked between the two men. "I heard about the other man who's gone missing. Amos Henderson. Have you had any luck locating him?"

"No." Gabe took her arm, guiding her across the street. "We searched for eight hours today. Shane, a few other deputies, and townsfolk will be starting again at sunup."

"Then they could search for Carson, also."

Stopping in front of the St. James, Gabe lowered his voice. "Let's learn all we can about his disappearance before making any decisions."

Pursing her lips, she met his gaze. "Of course, Sheriff."

Straightening her back, she marched up the steps, hesitating a moment when Shane rushed past her to open the door. Their gazes locked for a brief moment before Angela forced herself to look away.

She had to concentrate on her missing fiancé, not the man who'd walked away from her days after proposing. Following Thomas up the stairs to the third floor, her thoughts drifted back to earlier, when she'd approached Shane. He'd mentioned her being dead. Dead? Why would he have believed something so absurd?

"Miss Baldwin?"

Thomas stood next to the door, motioning for her to enter. Gabe and Shane followed.

"Sheriff, if you're going to be here, do you mind if I return to the front desk?"

"You go ahead, Thomas. I'll lock the room when we're finished."

"Where do you want me to start, Gabe?"

"The wardrobe, then the bedside table, Shane. I'll go over the rest. Miss Baldwin, why don't you have a seat?"

Back rigid, she tracked their progress. They were more meticulous than she'd been. Every drawer was searched, each corner of the wardrobe checked. Nothing was overlooked.

Stripping the bed, Shane's attention was drawn to what appeared to be dried blood. It was near the top, where the pillow would be. "Angie, did you notice this?"

Rushing to the bed, she stared at the brownish-red splotch on the sheet. "No. What is it?"

Shane noticed Gabe give a quick shake of his head. "Don't know for sure. We'll try to find out."

Gabe moved to the door, bending down to study a smudge. "Shane. Take a look at this."

Dropping the covers, he joined Gabe. "Dirt? Didn't think you allowed dirt in your hotel."

Angela stiffened at Shane's comment. "Do you own the St. James?"

Straightening, Gabe nodded. "I'm one of the partners. If we're finished here, I'll lock up and let Thomas know not to touch anything."

"What's next?" Angela asked as they walked downstairs and out the front door.

"Shane and a few of the deputies will start asking around. If nothing turns up, we'll look for him and Amos tomorrow. Do you have a picture of him?"

Fumbling in her reticule, she pulled out a photograph taken of the two of them before leaving Boston. "This is all I have on me. There's another one in my room of just Carson. I'll go get it."

"Wait. I want Shane to go with you. We don't know what happened to your fiancé. Until we do, I don't want to take a chance someone may be after you, also."

Angela cringed at the idea. "Me?"

"Right now, we don't know what's going on, Miss Baldwin. I'd appreciate it if you'd let Shane accompany you, then stay close until we figure this out."

Shane's eyes widened. "Gabe..."

"Come back to the jail when you get the picture. Bring Miss Baldwin with you."

Angela didn't object, hoping for a chance to be involved in the search. And discover more about Shane and why he'd left all those years ago.

Redemption's Edge

Shining Star held her baby boy close to her chest, rocking back and forth to sooth his whimpering. Wildfire Creek churned several feet away, overflowing after heavier than normal winter storms. Billy had told her the creek would slow, but would take longer than usual.

Billy. Humiliation slammed into her. He'd be worried, would already be searching for her. Shining Star didn't know why she'd run. When the last earthquake hit, the first she'd ever experienced, she grabbed her son, crouching in a corner of the house Dax had his men build for her.

The undulating earth felt different this time. As if the world would explode.

"Shining Star!" Billy's voice broke through the thick brush near the creek. Shifting to her knees, her son tucked tight against her, she stood.

"Billy!" She didn't move from the spot, her wary gaze moving, searching for any sign of danger.

Last time, bear had traveled closer to the ranch than usual, uncaring of the men with guns. A mountain lion tracked the women on one of their walks to the creek, the reason everyone carried a gun when leaving the safety of the ranch house. Had only a few days passed since the first earthquake?

"Shining Star!"

"Billy. I'm here!"

Rustling, similar to a bear charging its prey, had her moving away, then freeze. Billy burst into sight, storming toward her. Stopping a foot away, his concerned gaze traveled over her. He reached out his hand to cup her face, then dropped it, realizing it wasn't his right. Not until he confessed his feelings.

"You're all right?" Concern laced his words, his attention moving to the baby. "Both of you?"

"We are fine." She turned the child toward him, easing his anxiety.

Remembering Bram's last words, he pulled his gun. Raising it into the air, he fired twice. At her wide-eyed expression, his features softened.

"The others will know I've found you." Holding out his hands, he took the boy from her arms, cradling him to his chest. For an instant, the same intense feeling of possession gripped him. The child wasn't his. Not by blood. His mind and heart had never grasped the difference.

Shining Star had yet to name him, waiting until her grandfather and brother visited. It had been months without word, yet she refused to go forward.

"Billy! Shining Star!" Bram's voice reached them over the rushing water feet away.

The undergrowth crunched under the pounding of at least two sets of boots.

"Here!" Billy yelled. Seconds passed before Bram and Thane appeared, smiling when they saw Shining Star and the baby.

"Are you all right?" Bram asked.

"We are good, Bram MacLaren. Thank you for searching for us."

Thane lifted his gaze from watching Billy cradle the baby in one arm. "Everyone was worried when you weren't near the garden or in the house."

Chagrin showed in her features. "I am sorry. I should not have run."

Billy touched her arm before pulling it back to his side. "You had the baby to protect. I wish you'd stayed, but understand why you ran."

Lowering his head, he kissed the baby in his arms. The move startled him. By the looks on the others' faces, it surprised them. Clearing his throat, he handed the infant back to Shining Star.

"We should get her and the baby back to the house," Billy said, touching her elbow to encourage her to start moving.

"There's a decent amount of repairs to make." Bram scrubbed a hand down his face. "Thane and I will be staying to help." He wanted to check on Selina, confirm the wound had been treated.

Retracing their path, Billy stayed close to Shining Star. "Dax will tell you to head out. We have plenty of men to make the repairs."

Bram agreed with Billy. He'd stay long enough to check on Selina, and not a minute longer.

Chapter Ten

Bram held one of the posts for the porch steps, waiting for Bull to secure it in place. Ten more minutes, and the job would be finished. He wished the job would last longer.

This spot allowed him the perfect view into the living room where Rachel, Ginny, Lydia, and Selina rested from their injuries. Watching her, he could almost feel the agitation seeping from Selina. He knew how much she hated staying still.

None of the women had a choice. Dax's orders had been clear. They were to rest, not lifting a hand to help with repairs or straighten the house. He'd stared at each of them until they nodded in understanding.

After instructing Dax on how to treat her arm, Rachel had sutured the laceration on Selina's forehead, and rubbed salve on Lydia's and Ginny's wounds. They now relaxed, glasses of sherry near each one of them, as if they weren't hardworking ranch women.

The corners of Bram's mouth twitched when one of them said something, causing the others to burst into laughter. A pang of nostalgia gripped him. How many times had he seen the MacLaren women do the same at their Circle M Ranch?

When he, Thane, and Griff left for opportunities to expand the family brand, Bram had promised they would return every two years. It was a promise he intended to keep.

"I believe we're finished here, Bram." Bull wiped his brow, following his friend's gaze into the living room. A grin softened his often stoic features. "It could've been worse."

"Aye. Perhaps we've seen the last of the earthquakes."

Bull pursed his lips. "Perhaps." The tone of his voice held no reassurance.

"Papa. Can we go home now?"

Glancing down at his young son, Bull's face transformed, features softening. Bending down, he swept Josh into his arms.

"Should we get your mama?"

Vigorously shaking his head, Josh pointed toward the house. "She's in there."

"Then I guess we should fetch her." Nodding at Bram, Bull retreated into the house.

Bram watched, an odd sense of longing lodged in his throat. There'd been a time when he believed marriage and children were in his future. After his cousin, Cam, married Vangie Rousseau, Bram began distancing himself from his family.

Not intentionally. It seemed natural given that all those in his generation had married, and were having children. All except him. Rising early, training horses, then retreating back into his room after supper had become normal for him. Thane and their mother had been the only people to notice his gradual retreat.

It was then the idea of expanding Circle M began to grow. A year later, Bram and Thane accompanied their friend, Griffin MacKenzie, to Splendor.

Locating Thane with Dax and Luke repairing the back steps, they said their goodbyes. Bram considered checking on Selina once more, deciding against it. Plenty of people would keep watch on her.

Gathering their horses, they swung into their saddles, Bram taking one more glance through the front window. His eyes widened. Selina rested a hand against the window frame, her gaze meeting his. Lifting her other hand, she gave a slight wave.

Shane stood outside Angela's room, waiting for her to locate the photo of Carson. He couldn't stop watching her. The way she moved, the tilt of her head, her graceful hands opening a drawer to pick up the picture. She stared at it a moment before turning back toward him.

Hands fisting at his sides, he steeled himself against the pain of long ago. Nothing about seeing her again felt real.

"Here it is." Angela held it up for him to take.

Carson Bartholomew Winslow was a handsome man. Strong jaw, confident stance. Wearing a dark suit, one hand clasping a lapel, the other holding a black top hat.

"How tall is he?"

Angela rubbed fingers across her forehead, as if it was something she'd never considered. "Under six feet, but not much."

"What was he wearing the last time you saw him?"

"Dark pants and coat, similar to the photograph. But that was at supper last night."

Shane's lips thinned as he thought of the reasons Winslow might've gone missing. "Did you have an argument?"

"No. We never argue about anything." A sad smile tipped her mouth. "Our time together has been quite amicable."

Tilting his head, Shane studied her. The answer wasn't what he expected of a woman in love with her fiancé. It made him wonder, but not enough to ask. All he wanted was to find Carson alive. Then the couple could depart Splendor, leaving the agonizing memories where they should be—in the past.

"All right. Let's get to the jail. Maybe Gabe has found your fiancé."

Tugging on her lower lip, she didn't meet his gaze.

"Angie, are you ready to go?"

She lifted her face to his. "What happened?"

Shane's brows drew together. "We don't know yet. Won't until we locate him."

"I don't mean about Carson." She reached out to touch his arm, but he moved away, understanding her question.

Rubbing the back of his neck, Shane looked away. "I was told you traveled to visit your aunt and died of a fever. Your father said nothing more."

Shaking her head slowly, she fiddled with her reticule. "No. That can't be true."

"Believe it or not." He saw her shoulders slump and sighed. "It no longer matters. We've both moved on. You're engaged to a man from a good family in Boston. Let it go, Angie. I have."

Her shoulders slumped lower, but Shane ignored it. Taking her elbow, he guided her to the stairs, then outside. Neither of them spoke on the way to the jail. Opening the door, he motioned for her to enter.

Gabe sat at his desk, a man Shane didn't recognize across from him. He noticed Cash and Beau, both leaning against the walls.

"Shane, this is Cole Santori. Our newest deputy."

Shaking hands, Shane pulled out a chair for Angela, looking between the men. "This is Angela Baldwin. Her fiancé is missing."

Cash dipped his head. "Gabe told us. We'll do all we can to find him, ma'am. I'm Cash Coulter and this is Beau Davis."

"Thank you. I appreciate anything you can do to find him."

"Here's the picture of him." Shane handed it to Gabe, who studied it before passing it to the others.

"Several of the deputies are already looking for him, Miss Baldwin. If he's not found by tomorrow morning, we'll have a group of townsfolk who'll join the deputies. Including Cole."

"I can't imagine what happened to him. He's always so punctual, and well…"

"Well?" Gabe prodded.

"Dependable. If Carson says he'll be somewhere, he will be there. When he didn't meet me for breakfast, I knew something was wrong."

"Gabe told us you waited until after he missed your lunch appointment to alert us to his disappearance," Beau said.

"I believed he would've shown up by then. Thomas, at the St. James, did open Carson's room to confirm he wasn't ill. That's when I decided to seek out the sheriff."

When there were no other questions, Shane set a hand on the back of her chair. "If we're finished, I'll escort Miss Baldwin back to the hotel."

"No." Everyone's attention shot to Angela.

"No?" Shane asked.

"I want to help with the search."

The room quieted, Gabe the first to talk. "We appreciate the offer, but it's best if you let us do our job. We'll let you know if we find anything."

Lifting her chin, Angela squared her shoulders. "That is not acceptable, Sheriff. I intend to be part of the search. Either you'll allow me to join you, or I'll go on my own."

"You are a stubborn woman, Miss Baldwin," Gabe said, an edge to his voice.

"So I've been told. More than once, actually." Soft chuckles from the men in the room didn't switch her attention away from the sheriff.

Shane didn't like the look Gabe sent him, but stayed silent.

"All right. The deputies will be meeting at sunup tomorrow. You'll be joining Shane and whoever is with him. Will that satisfy you?"

Hesitating a moment, refusing to glance at Shane, she nodded. "That is quite acceptable."

"Will there be anything else?" Gabe asked.

"Not at this time." Standing, she met each of their gazes. "Again, I appreciate your help. I'll see you tomorrow, gentlemen."

Moving to open the door, Shane followed her outside. She wouldn't be going anywhere alone until they found her fiancé. Or the search ended, and she returned to Boston without him.

"You don't have to walk me back to the St. James." She kept her head high, almost marching toward the hotel.

Catching up, he kept pace, even when she tried to out distance him. "Carson is missing. We don't know what happened to him. One of the deputies, or I, will be escorting you around town until he's found."

"And if he's not? Found, I mean." Picking up her skirt, she hurried across the street. The sun dipping behind the western range told her how long she'd been at the jail.

"Are you hungry?"

Her stomach rumbled before she could answer. "A little."

Hurrying up the steps and into the hotel, she lifted a hand to Thomas, who smiled back. Turning to face Shane, she sucked in a breath. Being near him was much more difficult than she'd imagined. The past haunted her. She needed answers, and the only people who she could ask were her parents.

"Thomas, may we have a table?"

"Of course, Deputy Banderas. Follow me." Motioning her to go ahead, they took a few steps before stopping at a table close to the window.

"Will this be sufficient?"

"It's fine, Thomas. Thank you." Shane pulled out Angela's chair before taking his across from her. He wouldn't allow himself to get too close to her.

Glancing at the list Thomas gave them, she settled on venison steak, potatoes gratiné, and root vegetables. When the server took their selections, she shouldn't have been too surprised Shane ordered the same. It had always been that way with them.

"Are you married?"

Her question surprised him, but he didn't avoid answering. "No."

Eyes wide, she shifted toward him. "No? A fiancée, maybe?"

Letting out a breath, he glanced outside before meeting her interested stare. "Not married. No fiancée."

His words were clipped, a little strained. "Did you ever open the millinery shop you always talked about?"

Swallowing, she cleared her throat. "No." She didn't explain, although her eyes showed there was a story behind the answer. "How did you get to Splendor?"

Shrugging one shoulder, images of the years since he left home flashed before him. After being told Angela had died, he'd walked away from her home, from the town where they grew up. Over time, he carved out a different future. Alone. Without Angela.

"It was a long journey." He didn't say more, saved by the server placing plates before them.

Picking up her fork, sad eyes met his. "Won't you tell me?"

Shane shook his head. Angela would never hear the story from him. Not now. Not ever.

Chapter Eleven

Redemption's Edge Ranch

Opening one eye, then the other, Selina winced at the sharp spear of light slashing through the curtains. The bright rays told her it was past sunup, way past the time she needed to start her chores.

Forgetting about the injury to her head, Selina shot up, groaning at the slice of pain. Before her feet touched the floor, the door opened, Billy's younger sister, Margaret, entered, holding a tray.

"How are you feeling, Selina?"

"Better than last evening."

Setting the tray on the dresser, she picked up a plate with eggs and toast, handing it to her. "Rachel asked me to bring this upstairs for you."

"I could've joined you downstairs."

"She told me you'd complain about being served."

Snorting, Selina shifted on the bed, taking a bite. "Weren't you visiting a friend?" Balancing the plate on her lap, she touched her injury, wincing again.

"Billy came for me this morning. He wants me to stay close to the house for now." Sitting on a chair near the window, her mouth twisted. "He still sees me as ten instead of almost seventeen."

"Didn't you turn sixteen a couple months ago?"

"Yes, but that means I'm almost seventeen." Crossing her arms, Margaret rested into the chair. "Billy doesn't understand. Some of my friends are talking about getting married."

Gripping her fork so as not to drop it, Selina stared at her. "Married? Isn't sixteen a little young?"

"Not at all. Bram told me his parents were married about that age, as were his aunts and uncles. Of course, they were in Scotland when they met."

Her mouth curled into a grimace at the mention of Bram. "People used to marry young here in America."

"Exactly."

"*But* it's not as common as it used to be. Many women wait until they're closer to eighteen. I'm nineteen, and I have no intention of marrying for a long time."

Margaret giggled. "You have no intention of ever marrying."

Bram's image flashed before Selina. She shook her head, wincing again.

Rushing to her, Margaret studied the wound. "Are you all right, Selina?"

Waving her away, she forced a grin. "Yes. Seems shaking my head isn't a good idea until I've healed. Thank you for bringing me breakfast, but I need to get dressed."

"Why?"

Selina slid until her feet touched the ground. "That's a silly question. For chores, of course."

"No, you don't. Dax gave strict orders for you to stay in bed today *and* tomorrow."

Stilling, Selina rested her hand on the bed table. She might have a small amount of dizziness, but not enough to stay in bed.

"We'll see about that." Gaze fixed on her wardrobe, she took three steps before teetering. Reaching out, she stopped herself from falling against a wall.

Rushing forward, Margaret grasped her arm, helping Selina back to the bed. "Don't you dare move. I'm going to take your plates to the kitchen and make tea for us. Why don't I bring you some books?"

Selina muttered a word Margaret never heard from the other Pelletier women. Instead of commenting, she gave a half-grin before leaving.

Slumping against the headboard, Selina scowled. Staying inactive for one day would make her daft. Two days, and she'd be scheming ways to jump out a window.

In fact, she was already planning how to get Dax to soften his order. A few hours of rest would do her good. Two days in bed and she'd be raving.

Working with horses inspired Selina to get out of bed each morning. No matter what Travis asked of her, it wasn't a chore as long as it included a horse.

"Ugh..." Covering her face, she let out a deep sigh, feeling the throbs of a headache.

Rachel kept powder somewhere in the house to ease the pain, but Selina didn't want to see anyone. Not even Margaret, who walked back into the room, her arms laden with books.

"I didn't know what would appeal to you, so I brought several."

Selina knew she should be grateful, but her thoughts wouldn't leave the fact she'd been banished to her room. If it had been any of the men, Dax wouldn't have expected them to stay in bed for more than a few hours. They'd be handling their chores, being useful. Women weren't given the choice. Not unless they took it.

Her dour expression brightened. At nineteen, the decision to stay in bed or return to her chores should be hers.

"What time is it, Margaret?"

"Almost nine. Why?"

"Just wondering. Thank you for the books. If you don't mind, I'll rest for a bit before reading."

A smile lit Margaret's face. "Not at all. I'll come back up in an hour to see if there's anything you need."

Watching her close the door, Selina tossed off the covers, swinging her legs over the side of the bed. Dizziness assaulted her. Waiting for it to pass, she lowered her feet to the ground, steadying herself with a hand on the nearby table.

When certain she wouldn't collapse, Selina grabbed pants and a blouse from the wardrobe. It took longer than expected to dress. Feeling a wave of nausea, she lowered herself onto a chair, exhausted from the slight effort.

Refusing to admit Dax might be right, she reached out to snag her boots from a few feet away. Shoving into them, she straightened, sucking in air. Maybe she should've waited, but it was too late now. She refused to reverse her progress, undress, and climb back into bed.

Letting out a slow breath, Selina stood, determined to make it downstairs without falling. And without anyone spotting her.

Opening the door, she peaked up and down the upstairs hall. Satisfied, Selina grasped the handrail, taking slow, careful steps to the first floor. Stopping on the bottom step, she glanced around, listening for voices.

Hearing nothing, she took the last step. From this location, she could see into the living room, dining room, and down the hall to other bedrooms. No one appeared. Feeling a little dizzy, she gripped the rail, listening until the unsteadiness passed.

Again, Selina reconsidered the decision to leave her bed. Perhaps stubbornness had been stronger than her body's ability to heal. Turning toward the front door, she froze when it opened. Dax walked in, body tensing when he saw her. Worse, Bram followed a step behind.

"What was the lass thinking?" Bram gave a sharp shake of his head as he and Dax walked back to the corral.

"She wasn't. It's a problem with her."

Bram turned enough to look back at the house, toward Selina's second floor bedroom window. He knew she wouldn't be watching. Not after the verbal licking Dax dealt her. It wasn't too different from what his cousin,

Heather, used to endure after one of her poor decisions. As with his cousin, Selina's mood darkened, knowing Bram had heard the tirade. He heard a man who cared about a young woman under his protection. Hard and unyielding. In Bram's mind, nothing more than Selina deserved.

"Selina rarely considers consequences. She gets an idea into her head and acts." Entering the barn, Dax stopped, hands fisted on his hips. "Worse, she doesn't learn from her mistakes. It's the main reason we haven't given her more responsibility with the horses."

Mouth thinning, Bram gave a slow nod. "The lass is talented, and Travis is a fine teacher."

"Agreed. It's her maturity I question. She requires a firm hand, the same as some horses. Travis is excellent with the horses. One of the best I've ever seen. He's also hesitant to say the harsh words Selina often needs to hear." Dax dropped his hands, glancing at the house before meeting Bram's questioning gaze. "Bull did an excellent job teaching her how to work with the herd. He didn't soften his words. Would say the same to her as he would to any of the ranch hands."

"Perhaps Bull would be willing to do the same with the horses."

Dax chuckled. "He's too valuable working with the ranch hands. Besides, he's broken and trained horses when necessary, but it's not his strength." His gaze narrowed on Bram. "It is yours."

It took him a little time to get the meaning of Dax's words. When he did, Bram's eyes widened. "I'm not the best person to train the lass."

"You're the perfect person. I've watched you with Thane. Encouraging and tough."

"Aye, but Thane has been working with horses since he was ten. The lad is twenty-one. I've already taught him all I know."

"Not from what I've seen. We can talk about you and Thane another time. I want you to work with Selina."

"Dax..." Bram's voice trailed off as he wondered how to turn down the oldest Pelletier.

"You'll do a fine job."

"But..."

"By the end of summer, she'll have learned enough to take on a mustang by herself." Dax smiled, pleased with the solution. "You'll start with her day after tomorrow." Clasping Bram on the shoulder, he squeezed before leaving Bram in the barn, tight jawed and nostrils flaring.

Turned out only Bram thought Dax's idea ridiculous. Travis, Thane, and Bull agreed it was an excellent solution, and didn't hesitate to let him know.

One issue remained. Selina hadn't been told.

Dax refused to say a word to the stubborn woman until she had healed enough to join them at the corral. Bram didn't want to be anywhere close when she learned of the change.

Leaving the ranch well before sunset, he and Thane decided to ride through town on their way home. They'd done the same that morning, learning the town hadn't been affected by the earthquake, which injured the women. Gabe had also explained about another man going missing. Now there were two men who'd disappeared, leaving no clues as to what had happened.

Their offer to help had been appreciated, but declined. Vowing to explore every inch of town, three groups of men searched for a second day. Bram hoped there'd be good news when they reached the jail.

Dismounting, the brothers stopped on the boardwalk, taking a slow look around. There was little activity on an afternoon when the street would normally bustle with activity.

Pushing open the jail door, they were surprised to see one deputy. Bram removed his hat, nodding. "Mrs. Evans."

"Mr. MacLaren. How can I help you and your brother?" She offered a grim smile to Thane, motioning to the empty chairs.

Sitting, Bram's features turned severe. "Were they able to find the missing men?"

Letting out a frustrated sigh, she shook her head. "No. They searched for nine hours and found nothing."

"How can we help?"

"You'd have to speak with Gabe." She moved to the door, grasping the handle. "He and most of the other deputies are at the Dixie. I was just ready to lock the jail and join them.”

“We’ll go with you.”

Securing the door behind her, Beth crossed the street. “It’s been quiet since learning about the latest victim. Most are staying inside, with their guns close by.”

Bram and Thane exchanged glances before Bram spoke. “Do you mean the gentleman from Boston?”

Stopping outside the Dixie, she tilted her head to the side. “You haven’t heard?”

Bram’s gut clenched. Could there by a third missing person? “Heard what?”

“Rose Keenan, a server at the boardinghouse, didn’t arrive for work early this morning.” Biting her bottom lip, Beth glanced inside the saloon at Gabe and the other deputies before returning her gaze to Bram’s.

“There’s no sign of her anywhere.”

Chapter Twelve

Gabe watched the women seated at a table in a corner of the Dixie. He knew each one, and their association with Rose Keenan. Christina Boudreaux, Francesca O'Reilly Boudreaux, and Beauty DeBell were married to deputies. Georgina Wise, Carrie Galloway, and Amelia Newhall had traveled west with Rose and Francesca from New York almost two years earlier.

The six had formed their own search party after learning of Rose's disappearance. They'd checked the room she shared with Amelia at the St. James, spoken with employees of the Eagle's Nest and boardinghouse restaurants, and canvassed the businesses she often frequented.

Tearing his gaze from the women, Gabe looked between two of his men. "Cole, I want you and Shane to ride out to Redemption's Edge. It's the largest ranch in western Montana, owned by Dax and Luke Pelletier. Travis Dixon told them about Amos Henderson, but they don't know about Carson Winslow and Rose Keenan."

Shane shot a look at Angela, who stood by herself at the end of the bar. "Do you mind having someone escort Angela Baldwin back to the St. James?"

"Not at all," Gabe answered. "You know she won't want to leave until we decide how to continue the search."

Mouth twisting into a grimace, Shane nodded. "Cole and I will return as soon as possible."

"Come by the jail." Gabe saw Horace Clausen enter the Dixie, walking straight toward them. A moment later, Noah Brandt, Stan Petermann, Silas Jenks, and a few others shoved through the swinging front doors. "I've got to meet with the town leaders."

"We'll leave you to it." Shane didn't envy Gabe's responsibilities, not only to the town, but the various businesses he owned with his wife and Nick Barnett.

Stopping next to Angela, he explained Gabe's order. "One of the deputies will escort you back to the hotel. Don't leave the hotel for any reason, Angie. Odds are whoever took Amos and Carson, also took Rose."

"I understand."

"I'm serious about you not leaving the hotel. Make certain the door to your room is locked. Don't open it for anyone except Gabe, one of the deputies, or Thomas. I'll stop on my way out of town to request Thomas send supper to your room."

A brow rose, mouth twisting in controlled annoyance. "I'm capable of ordering supper, Shane. You have a job to do, so get to it. I'll wait here at the Dixie. Maybe Gabe will share whatever they plan next."

One corner of his mouth turned upward. "Nothing's changed with you, Angie."

Turning, he left to meet Cole outside on the boardwalk, but not before seeing her jaw drop. To her credit, she didn't yell after him, something she would've done when they were young, and he'd been stupidly in love with her.

"You ready, Cole?"

"My horse is at the livery."

"Mine, too. Let's get them saddled and ride out."

They walked the short distance to Noah's livery, taking the opportunity to look into each business, checking the narrow distances between the buildings. Shane had a hard time believing not a single clue had been left behind. No signs of a struggle, no torn clothing, or splatters of blood. He'd never known of such an efficient assailant.

Reaching the livery, they tacked up their horses, closing the gate behind them fifteen minutes later. Taking the trail north, Shane looked over at his companion. "Had you heard about the Pelletiers before today?"

"Not other than a few comments some townsfolk made during the search. I got the impression they're highly thought of."

"Biggest landowners this side of Big Pine. Many believe they own the largest spread in the entire territory. Dax is the oldest. Both fought for the Confederacy, receiving battlefield promotions. They're smart, strong leaders, and have worked hard for their success in Montana. Their ranch hands are loyal. They still have holdings in Savannah, Georgia, which I understand provides them with a decent amount of income. Can't swear to it, though. Besides Gabe, Nick, and Noah, I respect them more than any other men in the territory."

"I met Nick and Noah today." Cole thought of Nick Barnett, his formal attire, and broad smile. He sensed the man had steel for a backbone. Noah gave the impression of being relaxed. Looking closer, it hadn't been hard to spot the man's intensity, how he missed nothing. Both would be formidable enemies. Cole had no intention of ever getting on their bad sides.

"Gabe and Noah grew up together in New York. They left college to join the Union cause. Afterward, Gabe followed Noah to Splendor. They're tighter than brothers."

"Are you telling me not to come between them?" Cole asked.

"What you do is your business. Giving you some background is all." When the trail forked, Shane reined his horse to the left. "Riding to the right will take you toward a second ranch owned by the Pelletiers. The right of that is Dom Lucero's ranch."

"Lucero. I've heard that name."

"His wife, Josie, owns the Emporium with Doc McCord's wife, Olivia. He was the U.S. Marshal before building his ranch."

"Chan Evans took over as the U.S. Marshal?" Cole asked.

"He did, and he's darn good at his job."

"And married to Beth."

Shane grinned at the comment. Few men *weren't* attracted to Chan's wife. "Don't underestimate her. She's an ex-federal agent, and as good with weapons as most men."

Rounding a bend, the large Pelletier ranch house came into view. Past them were a few other smaller homes, a bunkhouse, and two barns. As they approached, a tall man with dark hair stepped onto the porch, raising a hand in greeting.

"That's Dax. We won't stay long. I want to get back to town before Gabe heads home for the night." Reining up, Shane slid to the ground. "Dax."

"Shane." Dax's piercing gaze landed on Cole.

"This is our newest deputy, Cole Santori." Following Shane up the steps, he grasped Dax's outstretched hand.

"Come inside. I'll get coffee, then you can tell me what brought you out here so late in the day."

Cole glanced around, impressed at the welcoming feel of the house. Not ostentatious, as he'd expected. The rooms were large, lived in, with comfortable furniture. As he turned, a tall woman with auburn hair and hazel eyes came toward them with a tray.

"Hello, Rachel."

"Shane. Glad to see you."

"This is Cole Santori, our new deputy."

Removing his hat, he made a slight bow. "Nice to meet you, ma'am."

"It's about time Gabe hired more men." Setting the tray down, she handed each of them a cup filled with coffee. "Would you care for sugar or cream?"

Shane shook his head.

"Black is fine with me, ma'am," Cole answered.

"Please, call me Rachel. Dax will be right back. He's getting Luke." Sitting down across from them, she studied the new deputy, but turned her attention to Shane. "It's a little late to ride out, isn't it?"

"Yes, but we've got news you'll want to hear."

The sound of the back door closing had the deputies standing, waiting for Dax and Luke to join them. Cole studied the two men. Similar in many ways, yet with distinctive differences. Luke had an easy smile, while Dax's took more effort. Approaching, Luke held out his hand to Shane, then Cole.

"Dax said Gabe just hired you. About time he added more men."

Cole shot a look at Rachel, both smiling at the exact comment she'd made a few minutes earlier. "Good to meet you."

Motioning for them to sit, Dax lowered himself next to Rachel, draping an arm over the back of the sofa. "Tell us why you rode out."

Shane set down his empty cup, and leaned forward. "You know Amos Henderson disappeared?"

"We heard," Luke answered. "Has he been found?"

"No. What you don't know is another man is missing. His name is Carson Winslow. He came to Splendor several days ago with his fiancée. Disappeared the day after Amos. Today, a third person went missing. Do you know Rose Keenan?"

Rachel jumped to her feet, her gaze moving between Shane and Cole. "I do. I'm the reason Rose came to Splendor." Dax grabbed her hand, tugging her down beside him. "What happened?"

"We don't know," Shane said. "When Rose didn't show up for work this morning, Suzanne reported it to Gabe. A search of her room, and the town, found nothing."

Shaking off Dax's hold, Rachel stood. "I can't stay here while Rose is missing. I need to ride to town."

Dax stood to stare down at her. "That's not going to happen. If you want, we'll head in tomorrow, but not tonight."

"He's right, Rachel," Shane said. "We had three groups of men searching, plus a group of women and all the deputies. Over thirty people."

"Nothing was found?" Luke asked.

Shane shook his head, disgust in his voice. "No. We have three missing people, and not one clue to help us find them. We've talked to everyone in town, searched each building, house, and business. No one saw anything."

"We'll get some men together and join you in town tomorrow morning." Luke rose, along with Shane and Cole. "Maybe our men will see something the others missed."

"We're open to any help offered." Shane shook hands before heading to the door with Cole. "No matter when you arrive, go to the jail. One of the deputies will be there. Unless something's changed, we'll be starting out a little after sunrise."

Catching a last glimpse of Rachel's ashen face, Shane's determination strengthened. They had a deranged person taking people off the street, leaving no tracks or evidence of what happened.

Hit gut told him they were being hidden away somewhere. Still alive. He couldn't prove it, but whenever he went against his instincts, he'd been sorry.

Riding faster on their return trip to town, Cole summarized what they knew about the people who'd been taken. "I don't see any connection. An original resident who returned to town recently. A businessman from Boston who'd never been to Splendor. A single woman who worked at the Eagle's Nest. The first is older, retired. The second is in his late twenties, successful, from a wealthy family. The third, a school teacher by education, single, from a working class family. What ties them together?"

"Nothing that I can see." Shane had met Amos several times, seen Carson once or twice, and knew Rose through her connection with Suzanne, May Covington, and Francesca. He couldn't speak for Carson, but Amos and Rose were good people, the type you wanted to call your friend.

"What does anyone have to gain by taking them?"

"I don't know," Shane replied, the answer haunting him.

Only one type of person came to mind, and the thought scared him.

Deranged, detached, with no concern for human life, including his own. The most dangerous person to walk the earth. A monster with nothing to lose.

Chapter Thirteen

MacLaren Ranch

Bram sipped coffee, looking at the other three men around the kitchen table. As the sun rose over the eastern range, the conversation focused on the events of the day.

Not much changed from one morning to the next, and the chores stayed the same. The differences now centered on the potential for more earthquakes, and whoever had taken three people off the streets of Splendor.

"I doubt he'll come this far from town."

Thane picked at his eggs, an odd occurrence for someone who was always hungry. "Are you certain it's a man, Bram? Could it not be a woman?"

Pausing a moment, he stroked his stubbled jaw. "She'd have to be a large lass, capable of subduing a man as large as Amos. According to Shane, Carson Winslow is close to six feet tall. He belonged to a boxing club in Boston."

"Does it have to be one person? Could've been a man and woman, or two men." Vince tapped his fingers on the tabletop, staring at the contents of his coffee cup.

Kev's jaw ticked before he spoke. "Where could three people be hidden for several days? If they're dead, surely there'd be some tracks or signs of a struggle. I remember when a rancher was kidnapped not far from our farm in Missouri. His family received a ransom note within hours."

Vince nodded, his hand clenching next to the cup. "They paid the money, but the outlaws killed him anyway." Lifting his head, he looked at Bram. "Have they gotten a demand for money?"

"Not that Gabe has shared with anyone. Be alert, and stay close enough to see each other." Finishing his coffee, Bram stood, Thane doing the same. "We're riding straight to the Pelletier ranch this morning. We plan to fulfill the contract for Fort Connall today, and leave early. You boys are taking on more than your share of work. Thane and I will be here until Dax decides which day we leave."

Kev pushed up from the table, setting his cup in the sink. "We can handle the chores here, Bram. Don't worry about helping out until you return from delivering the horses."

"Kev's right. We've been working for weeks on our own." Vince followed Kev to the sink, turning to lean his weight against the counter. "The additional hired hands you mentioned would be good once the herd is delivered."

Bram studied the brothers, pride surging. Kev and Vince were two of the most loyal ranch hands he'd known. They were the type of men Dax and Luke would hire within minutes of meeting them.

"Let's see how it goes today, and what else the Pelletiers want us to finish before leaving." Stepping onto the back stoop, Bram looked back at Kev and Vince. "Stay vigilant, lads."

Selina couldn't wait to get outside. She'd dressed and waited in the living room for Rachel to check her head wound until almost mid-morning. Pronouncing Selina well enough to continue her chores, Dax gave permission for her to meet the men at the barn.

She'd hoped to start back with chores the day before, but Shane's visit had changed everyone's plans. Rachel, Dax, Luke, and a few men had ridden out before sunrise, returning late yesterday afternoon. There'd been no smiles, no lively conversation over supper. It had been as Shane and the new deputy said. Whoever took the three had left no clues, nothing for the searchers to follow.

Pulling herself from the disappointing news, Selina rushed outside, she came to an abrupt stop. Travis spoke with Bram while Thane worked with a horse in the corral. Selina had hoped the MacLarens wouldn't be working today. She should've known better. They needed to break a couple more horses to fulfill the contract, then plan for the trip to Fort Connall.

Selina hadn't told anyone, not wanting to curse the idea, but she hoped to be included. Travis might allow it, but Dax would be much more cautious. Her going along made sense. It would leave another man to work with the cattle.

Seeing Travis walk off, she headed straight toward the barn, not acknowledging Bram as she passed. She'd almost reached the barn entrance when he called after her.

"We need to talk, lass."

Without turning around, she waved a hand in the air. "Later."

"Nae. We'll talk now." The harsh tone of his voice had her stopping. When he came up beside her, she steeled herself for whatever he might say, but more from the impact his closeness created.

The jolt of awareness made her uneasy, wishing he'd stand farther away. It had been almost unbearable when he'd held her after her injury from the earthquake. She'd wanted to squirm out of his arms, put as much distance between them as possible. Today was no different.

"Hurry up. I have chores to do."

"Aye, you do. You'll be working with me from now on."

Eyes wide, she shook her head. "I work with Travis."

"Dax made a change. You and I will be working together."

Without answering, she whirled around, stomping into the barn and toward Travis. "Is it true?"

Setting down the harness he'd been repairing, he met her angry gaze. "About working with Bram? Yes. Dax made the decision yesterday."

Crossing her arms, she shot a glare over her shoulder. "I will *not* work with him."

"Best if you speak with Dax about it. Don't believe it will help, though. He's already let the ranch hands know about his decision."

Throwing her head back, Selina's groan could be heard throughout the barn. "He's impossible."

Stifling a grin, Travis forced a blank expression. "Dax or Bram?"

"Bram, of course. Can't you talk to Dax? Change his mind?"

Setting aside the harness, Travis leaned against a stall. "Won't do any good. Dax told me of his decision before he ever spoke with Bram. He has his reasons, Selina. Maybe you should trust him."

An odd sound emanated from her mouth before she whipped around to face Bram, hands fisted at her sides. "You aren't as good as Travis."

Feeling a hand on her shoulder, she turned to see Travis's hard glare. "You be careful what you say. Bram is as good as any man I've ever seen. You'd be wise to open your mind and learn from him." Dropping his hand, he walked past them and out of the barn.

Neither spoke, each sizing the other up. Selina's face showed confusion at Dax's decision, and agitation at Bram's presence. Bram's features were bland, showing nothing of how he felt about the change.

Breaking the silence, he motioned toward a wall of tack. "Get a harness and rope. Meet me at the corral." Turning to leave, he stopped at her reply.

"Travis always brings the tack."

"It will soon become clear I'm not Travis, lass. Meet me outside."

He would've chuckled at the disbelieving look on her face, but didn't believe she'd appreciate it. Bram understood her frustration at the change. She'd become comfortable with Travis, trusted the man's instincts and instructions. He hadn't expected her to be happy about it, but didn't anticipate the hostile reaction.

Stepping on the lower rung of the fence, he rested his arms on the top rail, watching Thane stroke the horse's neck. Billy Zales had already slid the bridle on the young mare, waiting for Thane to swing onto the animal's back. Like Billy, Thane preferred to start bareback, calming the horse before cinching on a saddle.

Coming up to stand within feet of Bram, Selina watched the action in the corral. After years of breaking wild horses, Thane presented a calm grace evident in few wranglers.

With a sharp nod, Thane mounted the animal, taking the reins from Billy's outstretched hand. The air stilled around them, no one moving, including the horse. Without warning, the mare flew into the air, back arching in a move to dislodge the weight on her back.

Selina held her breath, as she did each time a rider mounted a wild horse. A surge of excitement whipped through her when the mare continued to buck. Thane remained on top, his body adjusting with each shift of the horse.

Gripping the top rail of the fence, Selina imagined herself on the mare's back, could almost feel her body undulating the same as Thane's. Closing her eyes, her fingers tightened on the rail, the same as if she were the one holding the reins.

Hearing the yelps and shouts of the men, her eyes popped open, the rapid beating of her heart slowing. Thane guided the quieted animal around the corral, talking in a soft voice while gaining the mare's trust.

"The lad has a gift."

Bram's voice drew her away from the corral to the man beside her. Forgetting her hostility toward Dax and his decision, she gave a slow nod.

"Yes, he does."

"Most can learn those skills. You do not have to be born with them."

Releasing her hold on the fence, she faced him. "An inborn sense of what to do can't be learned."

"Believing in your natural instincts is important. You have good instincts, lass. What you lack is experience."

Brows furrowing, her breath caught, wondering what Bram might be trying to tell her. "That's because Travis is cautious about letting me break the horses."

"There are times when less restraint is important for learning."

Selina licked her lips, working to staunch a wave of excitement. "Are you saying you'd let me try to break one of the horses?"

"I've not watched you enough to know." Walking past her, Bram opened the gate for Billy.

"Wait!" Her voice held a plea, stopping him from following Billy into the barn. "What does that mean?"

Studying her expectant features, he let out a sigh. "The contract has taken all our efforts. I've never seen you on a wild horse during this time."

"Because Travis decided I'd hold up the work."

"Was he right?"

Unable to hold his penetrating gaze, she stared down at her well-worn boots. Was Travis right to keep her off the wild horses? Did he believe her too green to be useful? She didn't want to voice the answer, but understood Bram wouldn't allow her to hide from the facts.

"Yes, he was." Without looking at him, she turned, hurrying away.

"Selina, wait." He didn't rush to join her, allowing time to get her thoughts in order. Bram had seen the flush in her cheeks, the embarrassment she tried to hide.

She was a proud woman, allowing few to see any weakness. He understood. Being accepted into a job dominated by men would deter the most confident of women. Even if their skills were equal, few would be hired when a rancher had the choice of an able-bodied man.

Stopping a foot in front of her, he waited until Selina met his gaze. "There's no shame in not being ready to break horses, lass."

She snorted out her disbelief.

"There's only shame in not continuing to work hard, or use the talent God gave you. Quitting on your dream won't make you happy."

Surprise registered on her face. "You think I have talent?"

Features softening, a smile tilted the corners of his mouth. "Aye, lass. You have many talents."

"If you can see them, why can't Dax or Luke?"

"They're burdened with great responsibilities. Their job is to generate work for dozens of men and women on the ranch. They don't always have the time to stop and take stock of the talents each person possesses."

Shoulders slumping, the hope of a moment before began to fade. "If that's true, what can I do? They've already made up their minds."

"Nae, lass. Dax wouldn't have asked me to work with you if they didn't believe in your abilities."

Eyes wide, she took a small step forward. "Do you really think so?"

"Aye, I do. After lunch, you're going to learn what's required to prove how valuable you are to Redemption's Edge."

Chapter Fourteen

Selina couldn't contain her excitement, legs bouncing under the table, fingers drumming on the arm of her chair. She hoped no one noticed.

The lunch Ginny and Lydia prepared had gone almost untouched. After a few bites of her biscuit and a couple bites of stew, Selina sat back. Her stomach churned at the prospect of what Bram planned.

To fulfill the Army contract, there were two more horses to break. Both mares, and small in stature. Less than fifteen hands. From what she'd observed, they were less agitated than the horses who'd come before them. Did she dare hope Bram would give her a chance to break one of them?

"You're not eating, Selina." Ginny's comment broke into her thoughts. "Does the food not agree with you?"

"It's wonderful, as always. I'm just not very hungry."

Today, the table held just four adults, or would've if Rachel hadn't decided to work in the garden with Shining Star. Bull and a couple ranch hands had carried a large part of stew and basket heaped with biscuits to the bunkhouse. All the men and children had decided to take advantage of the good weather to eat outside. Selina understood. She wished the women would've decided the same.

"If you'll excuse me, I'll clean up the kitchen before meeting Bram at the corral." Grabbing her plate, Selina picked up dishes in front of the other women.

"We can clean up," Ginny said. "Why don't you visit with Rachel and Shining Star for a few minutes before meeting Bram. Maybe it will cheer Rachel up a little."

"She took the news of Rose's disappearance hard," Lydia answered. "After several searches, there's no information on what happened to those abducted."

"If you're sure you don't need help in the kitchen."

Ginny waved her hand in the air. "We're fine. Go on, Selina."

Hesitating no longer, she set her dish in the kitchen sink, and rushed through the newly repaired back door. Slowing as she approached the large garden, she watched Shining Star settle her baby in a basket, tucking a blanket around the tiny form.

Billy had been tasked to protect Shining Star, a Blackfoot woman, from possible Crow raiders. Now he protected her baby boy. A boy who remained unnamed.

Selina had heard Billy, Dax, Luke, and Bull talk a few nights earlier about making the trip to the Blackfoot village. If Chief Running Bear couldn't travel to the ranch to name the child, they intended to take Shining Star and her baby to him.

"Do you need help?" Selina knelt down next to Rachel, who busied herself by pulling weeds choking a section of vegetables with her good right arm. The injured left arm needed several more days to heal.

Next to Rachel was the 1866 Winchester rifle Dax insisted his wife keep close by. A few feet away was the double-barrel scattergun Billy convinced Shining Star to carry when he wasn't with her.

Leaning back on her haunches, Rachel swiped moisture from her brow. "Thank you, Selina, but we're almost finished. It certainly is a beautiful day."

Tilting her head back, she sighed. The deep blue sky, marked by a few scattered puffy, white clouds, never failed to impress her. "Yes, it is."

"How are you doing with Bram?"

Selina's gaze whipped back to Rachel. "You knew about Dax's order?"

"He told me last night. I wouldn't have argued with him about it. From what I've observed, Bram is an excellent trainer."

"Of horses or people?" Selina couldn't keep the resentment from her voice. Even with the anticipated hope of getting on the back of a wild horse, she still didn't quite trust the Scotsman.

"Both. I do hope you'll give him a chance. He may allow you to take chances Travis would not."

"Perhaps. There are only two horses left to break for the contract. Both are more docile mares. Maybe he'll let me try one of them."

A high-pitched chirping sound captured their attention at the same time Shining Star grabbed the basket, rushing toward them. Eyes wide, she opened her mouth to speak when they heard the sound a second time.

"We must go." The fear in Shining Star's voice had them reaching for their weapons. An instant later, rustling in the bushes not fifty yards away spurred them into a run.

Reaching out, Selina took the scattergun from Shining Star's hand. Stopping, she turned to face the anticipated danger. "Get into the house."

"Selina, come with us!"

"I will, Rachel. Once I make sure whoever is out there doesn't come closer." Raising the shotgun, she pointed it toward the thick brush. Taking slow steps backward, her focus never left the spot where she expected someone to appear.

When the heel of one boot hit the steps, she steadied her aim.

"Selina, get inside." At Dax's firm voice, she lowered the gun.

Before she could pass him to enter the house, two horses with riders came toward them.

"Running Bear," Dax called out, lowering his own rifle. "Luke, get Billy and Bull. Running Bear and Swift Bear have arrived."

Shining Star sat on a chair in a corner of the living room, cradling the baby boy in her lap. Billy stood behind the chair, a hand resting on the back. Across the room, Running Bear and Swift Bear sat stiffly on a sofa, their discomfort evident. Dax and Luke had taken seats on two chairs, while Bull leaned against a wall. After an hour of discussions, there'd been no resolution about the baby, and Shining Star's possible return to the Blackfoot village. Nor had a decision been made on naming the child.

Dax cleared his throat, meeting Running Bear's impassive gaze. "Shining Star is welcome to stay at our ranch, but her desire is to return to her people. Is that not a reasonable request?"

Out of respect, Running Bear met Dax's gaze, but didn't respond. Minutes passed before Shining Star stood, pressing the baby to her chest.

"I will speak."

"Shining Star?" Billy stepped from behind the chair, placing a hand on her shoulder.

Without pulling her attention from her grandfather, she straightened her back. "I will speak, Billy Zales."

With a reluctant nod, he dropped his hand, taking a step away. "All right."

"Grandfather, I would ask for my son to have a Blackfoot name. This I ask of you because he is of your blood, and the blood of our ancestors. It is a warrior's story. A story I want my son to know." Her gaze shot to her brother before returning to her grandfather.

Swift Bear had said little since arriving, other than greeting his sister and taking a brief glance at his nephew. A softness shown in his eyes before an apology flickered in them. The knowledge her brother wouldn't support her desire to return to her people created a deep frisson in her heart. At that moment, Shining Star knew she was alone, except for one person.

The man who now stood behind her had never wavered in his responsibility to her. Although she'd kept her own feelings hidden, she knew Billy loved her, wanted her as his own.

Chin raised, Shining Star stood her ground, refusing to sit down or back away until her grandfather spoke his decision. Tightening her hold on the baby, she forced breaths in and out, keeping her gaze focused straight ahead.

Without standing, Running Bear gave a slow nod. "You have spoken well, granddaughter. From now on, your son will be called Spirit Bear. His history will be our history. His story our own."

Tears welled in her eyes, but she forced them back, praying her voice didn't falter. "Thank you, Grandfather. Spirit Bear is a strong name for a future warrior."

As with Swift Bear, something flickered in her grandfather's eyes before disappearing. Standing, Running Bear motioned to his grandson to do the same, his attention moving to Dax.

"We will leave now."

"What about Shining Star?" Dax asked, seeing the stricken features on the young woman's face.

"Her future is here, with you, Dax Pelletier. And with you, Billy Zales."

Watching her family walk outside to their horses, Shining Star couldn't move. Nor could she stall the tears a second longer. She allowed them to fall, hands gripping her baby as quiet sobs racked her small form. They hadn't said goodbye, didn't acknowledge her in any way after Running Bear had named her son.

Feeling strong arms wrap around her, she sobbed into Billy's chest, unashamed at the show of emotion. The reality she might never see her family again ripped open her heart.

Pulling back, she raised her head, meeting Billy's unwavering gaze. When he lifted a hand to sweep hair from her face, she experienced a new type of longing.

Bram stood next to Selina and Thane, watching the two Blackfoot ride out. Shining Star wasn't with them. He knew little about the tribes east of California, but the fact they'd left her behind made their decision clear. The young woman and her baby would be staying at Redemption's Edge.

"Suppose we should get back to work. Selina, why don't you cut one of the last two mares from the herd and move her into the corral." Bram walked off without further comment.

She looked at Thane, eyes bright with excitement. "Did I hear him right?"

"You sure did. I'll get the gate."

Bram stopped at the barn, turning in time to see the huge smile on Selina's face before she rushed toward him.

Without a word, she walked out the back of the barn, whistling for Honey.

Taking little time to tack up the mare, Selina swung into the saddle. The smile never left her face as she rode out to fetch the wild horse. There were two in the corral. The last of the animals destined for the trip to Fort Connall.

Retrieving the rope from her saddle, she studied the two mares. They were about the same size, with similar coloring. Deciding on the one with black points, she approached it with a sense of confidence, using the rope to move the mustang to action.

Her mare had been trained to work with cattle, was as good as any at cutting out strays. The last year, she'd become accustomed to doing the same with the wild horses.

Over that time, Selina and Honey had become partners, doing whatever Travis asked. Cutting out a mustang to be broken had become her role. Once in the corral, she'd move outside, letting one of the men do the rest of the work. Today, she hoped to be the one staying, the one to get on the back of the horse.

Herding the mare into the adjoining corral, she rode to the gate on the other side. Bram stood next to Thane. Neither moved as she'd expected.

"Who's going to give her a try?" Selina asked, her heart thumping with hope.

Crossing his arms, Bram studied her. After a moment, he turned to Thane. "You're inside the corral." When

Thane picked up a halter, he turned toward Selina. "You ready?"

Swallowing the knot of fear mixed with anticipation, she met his gaze. "Ready for what?"

"You wanted a chance to break a horse, lass. Well, your chance is here."

Chapter Fifteen

Relaxed, yet on alert, Thane held the mare in place for Selina. It had been easier than they expected to calm the horse before sliding the bridle in place. Instead of a saddle, Selina had decided to ride bareback, the same as Thane.

Neither of the MacLarens had encouraged her to do so, but Bram was determined to let Selina determine how to mount the mare. If she stuck, it would be cause for celebration. If not, she'd learn from it and move on. What she learned would be up to her.

Bram stood outside the fence, jaw tight, lips pursed. He'd never admit the fear he felt for Selina. It would destroy him if anything happened to her. How could he deny her a chance at her dream? He couldn't. The same as his family had encouraged his cousin, Heather, to become one of the finest horse women in California, he'd encourage Selina.

"What do you think?"

Bram hadn't noticed Dax come up beside him until he spoke. "The lass is ready up here." He tapped his forehead. "We'll see if she's ready here." Moving his hand, he tapped his heart.

"You're talking about how bad she wants it," Dax said, his attention never wavering from Selina.

"Aye. If the mare bucks her off, will she get back on? I've seen lads who talked a big story, but gave up after their arse hit the ground."

"She'll stick, Bram. No doubt in my mind."

"I agree. The lass has more grit than a lot of men."

"That she does." Bram hoped it would be enough to get Selina through her first ride.

Stroking the mare's neck, Selina closed her eyes, blocking out everything around her except the horse. Inhaling and exhaling, she envisioned gripping the lush mane with her left hand before swinging atop the mare's back.

From watching the others, she expected a few seconds without reaction as the mare became aware of the extra weight. Her next vision was of her being bucked upward. Gripping the reins and thick strands of mane, thighs clamping around the horse's girth, the image changed to her own body adjusting to stay atop the animal.

"You ready, Selina?" Thane's quiet question pulled her away from the vision.

Staring down at her boots, she took a couple more deep breaths. The same as Bram, Thane, and Travis, she didn't wear spurs, preferring to use the heel of her boots. Selina had no real objection to those ranch hands who preferred them. Each person was free to choose how to outfit themselves.

Hesitation over, she glanced at Thane before gripping the mane in a tight hold and swinging on the mare's back. Forcing herself to breathe, she waited for the storm to come. Seconds passed before the mare snorted, her front hooves raising into the air.

Landing hard, Selina felt her teeth rattle. Determined to keep her seat on the horse's back, her body relaxed, absorbing each buck. Thinking she may have succeeded, Selina lost her focus for a few critical seconds at the same time the mare soared into the air, whirling in a circle.

The move dislodged Selina. Her thigh muscles lost their grip, unable to hold her in place. Stopping abruptly, the mare reared back. Unable to stay on, Selina flew into the air, landing hard on her backside.

The landing jolted her entire body. Trying to sit up, Selina's head spun. In front of her, she saw two images of Thane standing in front of her. Blinking several times, she looked again. This time, the two images merged into one. In the distance stood the mare, rearing her head up and down in triumph.

"Are you all right, lass?"

Shifting her gaze from the mare to Bram, she swallowed a rush of humiliation. Selina wondered how many men saw her fly into the air to land in a heap on the hard ground.

"Let's get you up." Dax knelt on the other side of her, slipping his arm behind her back. Together with Bram, the two raised her up, holding on while she gained her footing.

"How's your head?"

Glazed eyes met Bram's. "It's fine. I want to try again."

He looked past Selina to Dax, who gave a slight shake of his head. If she were a man, Bram knew Dax would encourage him to remount and finish what he'd started. Lips thinning, he made a decision his partner wouldn't like.

"If you're thrown a second time, you're done for the day, lass."

Taking a step forward, she steeled her resolve. This was her chance to prove she deserved the title of wrangler. She might not be as good as the others, but walking away would confirm her defeat. Dax and Bram might never let her back on a wild mustang again.

"She won't throw me a second time." Hands clenching and unclenching at her sides, she nodded at Thane. A smile curved his mouth before he went after the mare. Billy joined him. Within minutes, they'd backed the horse against the fence, Thane grabbing the reins.

"We need to saddle this miscreant for Selina."

Billy chuckled, nodding in agreement. "I'll get it."

Selina waited for Thane to bring the mare to her. Out of the corner of her eye, she watched Billy leave the corral, returning a moment later with her saddle.

"I don't need it."

"You'll use it, lass, or you won't ride." Bram's unyielding command stopped the argument she'd been ready to voice.

Biting her lower lip, she tapped down the irritation building in her chest. Per Dax's order, Bram was now her boss, the man who would decide whether she'd join the others to break wild horses, or stand on the sidelines.

Blowing out a breath, she gave a curt nod, showing none of the annoyance she felt. She believed the rider should select their own gear, decide between bareback or a saddle, and whether they wore spurs.

Watching Billy saddle the dancing mare, Selina reminded herself how much more knowledge the men possessed compared to her scant experience. She had a lot to learn, and knew her attitude wasn't helping.

Before deciding she had to pursue her dream, she'd been more malleable, doing as everyone asked. Cleaning, laundry, cooking, and tending the garden took most days. Her respite had been the daily rides close to the ranch house. If someone joined her, they'd take trails north or south, spending at least an hour exploring areas she rarely saw.

Selina had woken one morning, knowing she couldn't face another day of working in the house. Begging clothes from Billy, she'd cinched the pants up with an old belt, tucking the oversized shirt inside.

Not even Dax seemed surprised when she'd announced her intention to work with Travis. The objections she'd expected never came. Dax and Luke had walked with her to the corral, spoke with Travis, then left her alone with the quiet wrangler. She'd learned a great deal, but had never been given the opportunity to break a horse.

Displeased at first, the change from Travis to Bram had been a blessing. The least she could do was accept his instruction, continue to learn from a man quite different than Travis.

The problem wasn't so much his orders. His nearness messed with her concentration, created a strange swirling feeling in her stomach. When he rode in from his ranch each day, her chest would squeeze, throat thicken. Unexpected reactions Selina had no idea how to handle.

Closing the short distance to the mare, she saw what appeared to be a smirk on the mare's face. Whatever the look was, it wouldn't stop her from taming the wild animal.

Grabbing a large amount of mane, she swung into the saddle. Not waiting for the mare to react, she dug her heels into the horse's sides. The reaction was swift.

The mare reared back as before, bucking, then whirling. This time, Selina was prepared. Gripping the saddlehorn, she hung on, refusing to be dislodged from the saddle.

Finishing a third rotation, the mare came to an abrupt stop, snorting. Selina tightened her hold and squeezed her thighs around the horse, ending her forward momentum. Letting out a relieved breath, she wasn't prepared for the next move.

The mare settled her weight on her strong front legs, hind legs kicking out. Repeating the action several times, the horse began to whirl again, twisting in the air before landing on the ground.

Body shifting in the saddle, Selina's self-assurance began to wane. Her damp palms struggled to get a solid grasp on the saddlehorn. Shouts of encouragement reached her ears, men's and women's voices praising her efforts, boosting her confidence.

Selina squared her shoulders, absorbing the mare's actions. Her body relaxed, moving in a fluid motion with the animal. When she thought the horse would never stop bucking, it stilled.

Blowing out hot bursts of air, the mare's hooves dug into the ground, the displeasure at not throwing Selina obvious.

"Don't move," Billy called. "Wait for her to realize you've won and she's lost."

"And be ready," Thane added. "The mare may try bucking you off again."

Holding the reins in one hand, the other hand clasped around the saddlehorn, Selina did as the two instructed. Heart pounding in her chest, she tried to tamp down her excitement.

When the mare failed to move for several minutes, Billy stepped closer. "Take her around the corral a few times. Let her get used to you being in charge."

For the first time since the mare had stopped bucking, Selina spared a glance to where Bram stood on the other side of the fence. Her breath caught at the look of approval on his face. Beside him, Dax offered the same, as did several of those standing around the corral.

Completing five rounds, Bram waved her toward the gate. "You've done well, lass. Bring her out and let's see how she does in a stall."

"Isn't it a little early to put her in the barn?" Selina had never seen them shelter a gelding or stallion after first breaking them.

"We'll leave her there a couple hours while Thane breaks the last horse of the contract. When he's finished, you'll tack her up by yourself."

Eyes wide, Selina slid to the ground, guiding the horse into the barn. "You want me to ride her a second time?"

"Aye, lass. Once I'm satisfied, you'll put her with the other horses we'll be taking to Fort Connall."

"I want to go." She blurted it out, surprising herself and Bram.

"Not this trip. Dax has already spoken with the men who will be going."

Guiding the mare into a stall, she closed the gate. "When do you leave?"

Bram watched the mare, pleased to see her accept the confinement. "Tomorrow."

"So soon?"

"We've a long way to go, and a deadline to make." Bram turned away, believing the conversation over. He always seemed to be wrong about Selina.

"I'll talk to Dax."

Placing fisted hands on his hips, he turned around to face her. He *did not* want her to go with them. There were too many unknowns and dangers on the trail, not to mention the threat from whoever had already taken three people.

"You're needed here, not on a drive that will take you away from the ranch for as many as four days."

Crossing her arms, she stomped past him. "We'll just see what Dax says."

Showing more bravado than she felt, Selina headed straight to Dax's office. Drawing the door open, she stopped. Dax, Luke, Bull, and Travis were huddling over the desk, staring at a large piece of paper.

"What is it, Selina?" Dax's voice sounded strained, and troubled.

Pursing her lips, she took a few steps forward, sensing someone at her back. Glancing behind her, she grimaced. Bram stood two feet away, his arms crossed, feet planted shoulder width apart.

"I want to go on the drive to Fort Connall tomorrow."

The four men around the desk answered at the same time. "No!"

"But—"

Dax held up a hand, stopping her. "The issue is closed, Selina. You'll stay here."

"You know I'm good enough to go."

Straightening, Dax's nostrils flared, features going rigid. "As I said, you are not part of the group going. We'll discuss future drives later."

Seeing his jaw tighten, Selina knew she'd pushed far enough. Whirling around, she shoved past Bram. Dax may have ordered her to stay, but that didn't mean she had to obey him.

Chapter Sixteen

Splendor

"No one's seen him in two days, Gabe." Dom Lucero set his hat on the desk, then scrubbed a hand down his face. "He left the herd to check on strays and never came back. My foreman, Mal Jolly, was with the men. They searched that day and the following. Mal's a pretty good tracker, but there were no signs of the boy."

Gabe lifted a brow. "Boy?"

"My guess is he's no more than sixteen. Real good worker, with experience on a ranch. Doesn't talk much. Fact is, we don't know anything about Charley. Showed up a couple months ago, starving, and darn near begging for a job. Mal fed him and assigned him a bunk."

"What's Charley's last name?"

"Jones. Don't know if it's his real name or not." Dom massaged the back of his neck, concern etched on his face.

"Describe him." Gabe wrote it all down. Close to six feet, sandy red hair, freckles, wiry.

"He has a birthmark right here." Dom pointed to a spot below his left eye. "Damedest one I've ever seen. Looks somewhat like a bear paw. Circle with four tiny ones. The whole thing is no larger than a dime."

Leaning back in his chair, Gabe studied the notes, jaw clenching at the idea their kidnapper may have extended his territory. "You know about the three people from town who've gone missing?"

"Josie told me. I would've come in to help, but it's spring roundup."

Gabe held up his hand. "We had plenty of people. Francesca and her women friends even formed a group. We talked to everyone in town, searched all the buildings and houses. Not a single clue as to what happened. Charley is the first person who's disappeared outside of town."

Standing, Gabe walked to the front window, staring out at Frontier Street. "I've extra deputies posted, and have hired a new one. At this rate, I'll need to hire more to find those who've been taken."

Joining Gabe at the window, Dom looked toward the Emporium, the shop his wife, Josie, and Olivia McCord owned. A ball of fear built in his chest.

"I'll be bringing Josie to and from town until the man has been found."

"Or men," Gabe said. "We believe the abductor has to be strong enough to overpower and drag a grown man a good distance from where they're taken."

"Could he have used chloroform?"

"Maybe. Could've just knocked them out. We couldn't find any signs of a struggle or marks indicating the victims were dragged away. Doc Worthington made a count of chloroform, laudanum, and other medications in the clinic. Nothing's missing."

Turning away from the window, Dom grabbed his hat from Gabe's desk. "I can send in some men to help search."

"I'd rather you use them to guard your ranch. Any chance you have someone who could ride over to the Pelletier ranch and let them know about your missing man?"

"I'll ride there myself after I get Josie."

"Appreciate it, Dom. Sorry about your man. I'll send a couple deputies tomorrow to talk to your men. Maybe someone will remember a detail that might help."

Drawing the door open, Dom stopped. "You know, there are a few people who live in the mountains. Most have probably come down for the spring to pick up supplies. Might be worth sending some men to talk to them. Those people see a lot that we don't."

"Hadn't thought of them. I'll talk to Cash and Beau. Those two would be the best at finding their cabins."

"And caves," Dom added before closing the door behind him.

Redemption's Edge

"Billy, are you ready for tomorrow?" Bull sat outside with the men, eating the chicken stew and biscuits the women had made. "This is the best stew yet."

Chuckling, Billy swallowed a mouthful. "You say that every night. We leaving at sunup?"

"We're getting an early start. With luck, we may be able to reach Fort Connall late tomorrow evening."

Tilting his head back, Billy looked up at a clear sky dotted with more stars than anyone could ever count. The sight never failed to make his heart stutter. The same as it stuttered each time his gaze landed on Shining Star.

The desolation on her face when Running Bear and Swift Bear rode away almost killed him. She knew, as did he, her family might never visit again. In his mind, it was their loss. Shining Star's beauty went deep. Few women possessed as big a heart or accepted others as they were. Everyone at the ranch loved her, would defend her with their lives, the same as with any of the Pelletier women.

She'd become one of them. Even pregnant, and now with the baby, she worked as hard as any of the women. He'd never known anyone who faced each obstacle with unwavering grace. Never a mean word for anyone.

Recalling Bull sitting beside him, he swallowed down a bite of stew with tepid coffee. "Who all is going?"

"Travis, Bram, Thane, you, and me. Dax is considering having Tad go with us."

Billy snorted, scooping up another portion of stew. "Bet you suggested him."

"I did. He's been with us for years, knows the trail north, and has become a crack shot. Having him along would ease my mind."

"And give us one more man than we actually need." Billy held up a hand when Bull opened his mouth to object. "Which I believe is a darn smart idea."

Throwing back his head, Bull blew out a deep, throaty laugh, causing all eyes to land on him. "Darned if I don't think the same."

Settling down, Billy's features grew serious. "I heard Selina asked Dax if she could go with us."

"She did. He turned her down. Selina tried to argue, but Dax refused to listen. Bram was in the room, said she wasn't too happy about it."

"More than unhappy," Billy said. "She stormed around the barn, muttering to herself, not caring if anyone heard. Wouldn't surprise me if she tried following us."

Not much surprised Bull, but her going against Dax's order had him choking on his last bite of supper. "Selina surely isn't that stupid. Dax would never allow her to work the horses again if she goes against his order."

"Don't know about stupid, but she's stubborn to a fault. She isn't one to accept what she doesn't want. I'm certain she'll be considering trying to sneak out. It'd be best if we kept a lookout for her once we get on the trail."

Standing, Billy held his plate, cup, and utensils, looking toward the house. "I'm going to find Shining Star, see if she needs anything before she goes to sleep."

"Uh-huh," Bull muttered.

"What?"

Shaking his head, Bull's mouth twisted into a wry grin. "When are you going to tell her?"

Staring down at him, Billy's brows furrowed. "Tell her what?"

"That you love her."

Billy washed his dishes before heading to the small house Shining Star lived in with Spirit Bear several yards from the bunkhouse. From ten feet away, he could hear the baby crying, knew she'd already be comforting him.

Raising his hand to knock, Billy hesitated. Bull's words came back to him, the answer simple. No, he hadn't expressed his feelings to Shining Star.

He'd expected Running Bear to insist she return to the village. Instead, he'd left without a backward glance at his granddaughter, stunning everyone. No one more than Billy.

Shining Star allowing him to hold her had rendered him almost speechless. Whispering words of consolation, he'd assured her how much she was wanted at Redemption's Edge, how she and Spirit Bear would be protected, and what a wonderful future she'd have at the ranch.

What he hadn't said was he wanted to be the one to protect her. How he loved her more than his own life, and hoped to marry her.

Billy told himself she needed time to adjust to never returning to her village. What Shining Star didn't need was to hear his confession of love.

Deciding not to disturb her, he turned to leave when the door drew open.

"Billy Zales. You are leaving?"

Letting out a breath, he turned to face her. "I heard the baby crying and didn't want to disturb you."

"You could never disturb me."

His gaze narrowed on her face. Did he see a blush creep up her cheeks?

Standing aside, she motioned for him to enter. "Spirit Bear is asleep now."

He'd been in the house many times since Rachel and Lydia moved her in after the baby was born. Somehow, his presence this evening felt different.

"I can make coffee."

Billy recalled teaching her how to use the coffeepot. She'd been asking for days, determined to offer the women who visited something to drink. After demonstrating, it had taken her three pots before she'd been satisfied.

"I don't want you to go to any trouble, Shining Star." The smile he'd come to expect broke across her face.

"No trouble."

Watching her walk to the kitchen, he took a moment to study her. Head held high, shoulders squared, he couldn't help comparing her to his image of a princess. In a way, she'd grown up a princess as the granddaughter of the Blackfoot chief.

Billy had stopped by to tell Shining Star he'd be leaving at first light. Setting his hat on the small kitchen table, he again recalled Bull's words.

Did he have the courage to voice his feelings? He never considered himself a coward. Confessing his love had his entire body shaking. Maybe it would be best to wait until they returned from the fort, when there would be plenty of time to talk.

A grim smile twisted his mouth. They wouldn't need much time if she didn't feel the same. And if she felt nothing except friendship for him? Billy's heart twitched.

"Black?"

Her question drew his attention. "Yeah. Black is good." Taking the cup she held out, he hid a grin while she prepared her own.

Shining Star filled her cup halfway up, adding the same amount of milk, and several pinches of sugar. Stirring, she took a small sip, eyes sparking in pleasure.

"Satisfied?"

After a shy nod, she sat down at the table, motioning for him to join her. Instead, he set down his cup, pacing a few feet away. Stopping, he inhaled and exhaled several times, deciding now was as good a time as any to express his feelings.

Walking back to the table, he grabbed his cup, swallowing the contents. He wished there'd been whiskey, but coffee would have to do.

Watching him, concern etched the corners of Shining Star's eyes. "Are you all right, Billy Zales?"

No, he wasn't, but he wouldn't admit it. Not now, when he was about to bare his soul.

"There's something I need to say."

Lifting her chin, she set the cup aside. Placing both hands on the table, she started to stand when he shook his head.

"Please, stay seated. I think that would make it easier for me to get this out." Ignoring the worry on her face, he shifted to face her. Billy opened his mouth, then closed it. Throat dry, heart thumping hard against his chest, he fisted his hands at his sides. He had to get this said.

"There's something you need to know."

"Yes, Billy. What is it you want to say?"

"Well—" The one word was all he got out before the sides of the house began to shake, the wood floor rippling beneath his feet.

Grabbing Shining Star's arm, he tugged her up. "Get outside, and into the open. I'll get the baby."

"But—" Her hands gripped the side of the table when the rumbling increased.

"Don't argue. Get out...now!" Hoping she did as he said, Billy ran to the bedroom, scooping up the baby. Hurrying out, he'd just reached the front door when a loud rumbling shook the entire structure.

Cradling the baby to his chest, he huddled down when the roof cracked.

Outside, Shining Star watched the porch buckle, a moment before the entire roof collapsed.

Chapter Seventeen

A low moan began deep in Shining Star's chest, bursting into a scream when she dashed back to the house. Strong hands grabbed her, tugging her back as another, stronger quake ripped a long crevice in the earth yards from where they stood.

"It's too late." Bull's voice didn't stop her from trying to pull out of his grasp.

"Spirit Bear and Billy. They are inside," she screamed, a sob bursting loose.

"There's nothing we can do until the shaking stops." Dragging her back, Bull's gaze landed on Lydia.

Huddling yards away, she had an arm around their son, Josh, a hand resting on her stomach. They'd learned weeks before she was pregnant. His stomach twisted at the thought of anything happening to his family.

Fighting Bull's tight grip, Shining Star couldn't bear the thought of losing her baby, or Billy. "I have to go to them," she pleaded, twisting against him.

Swinging her into his arms, he walked toward Lydia, almost losing his balance when another tremble rocked the ground. Steadying himself, Bull dropped to his knees when another major rumble shook the earth.

Shining Star tumbled next to Lydia, tears streaming down her face. She stared at the house, seeing the entire structure slant to one side. Somewhere inside were Spirit Bear and Billy.

"You have to believe they're all right," Lydia said, rubbing a hand down Shining Star's back. "Look over there." She pointed to Dax and Luke with a group of ranch hands. All held shovels, picks, or ropes. "They're waiting for the quake to calm, then they'll do everything possible to get Billy and your baby out."

The remaining women and children joined them, faces marked with dirt. Patrick Pelletier, Dax and Rachel's five-year-old son, wrapped both arms around his younger brother, James. Both of their faces were streaked with tears, as were those of Coop Pelletier, Luke and Ginny's four-year-old boy. Rosemary Masters held her year-old boy, Graeme. Her husband, Dirk, the other Pelletier foreman, stood with the other men outside Shining Star's damaged house.

Rachel leaned toward Ginny. "Can you watch Patrick and James? I want to be ready to help when the men bring out the baby and Billy."

"You do what's needed. I'll take care of the boys."

It seemed the worst of the earthquake had passed by the time Rachel walked the short distance to join the men. Moisture coated her hands, trepidation grinding in her stomach. Billy was like a son, a boy she'd watched grow into a remarkable man. Losing him would hurt a great many people, especially his younger sister, Margaret. Rachel was glad they'd allowed her to stay with friends on the other side of Splendor for a few days.

Stopping next to Dax, she threaded her fingers through his, breath catching at the damage before them. The house still swayed from the impact of the quake.

Squeezing her hand, Dax let go, turning to those around him. "We'll take it slow. Luke, Bull, and I will start at the front while the rest of you stay back. If the house has stabilized, I'll call you forward. Bull will let you know what to do." After one last look at his wife, Dax strode to the porch.

Rachel knew the odds of finding life in the broken structure were slim. The earthquake had hit hard and fast, without warning. No small tremors to announce its coming. Knowing Billy, he'd ordered Shining Star outside, staying to grab the baby. If he'd lived through the quake, she knew the baby would be safe.

"Billy Zales is alive."

Rachel shifted to see Shining Star beside her. "How do you know?"

"I know. He has Spirit Bear in his arms. They are both alive."

Opening her mouth to respond, she clamped it shut as the front door was torn from its hinges. Reaching out, she took Shining Star's hand in hers.

Dax went in first, followed by Luke, then Bull. It seemed as if an hour passed before Bull appeared in the opening. Rachel guessed it was minutes.

"Tad, Dirk. We need your help."

When Shining Star tried to follow them, Rachel grabbed her arm. "You must trust they know what they're doing."

Hearing the angry cries of a baby, she ripped out of Rachel's hold. Rushing forward, Shining Star stopped when Bull stepped carefully through the debris. In his arms was her baby.

Sobs tore from her lips when he settled Spirit Bear in her arms. Clutching the restless boy to her chest, pained eyes met Bull's.

"Billy Zales?"

Instead of answering, he looked at Rachel. "You'll need your bag. Tad is getting a wagon ready."

Bull didn't have to tell her what they'd found was bad. Rushing toward the house, Travis pulled her back, stopping her progress.

"I'll go. Where is the bag?"

"In the closet off the kitchen."

"Don't follow me, Rachel. I'll bring the bag to you."

Unable to wait, she hurried to where the men were carrying Billy outside on a makeshift

stretcher. Setting him in the back of the wagon, she climbed inside. When Shining Star attempted to join her, Dax held her back.

"You'll ride on the seat with Tad. Bull and I will be in the back with Rachel. Do you need anything for the baby?"

"Here." Lydia handed Dax a satchel. "Take this with you."

Swiping at a lone tear, Shining Star stared down into Billy's swollen face. His ripped clothing exposed long gashes on his chest, arms, and legs. Rachel did her best to doctor the wounds, knowing suturing would have to wait until they reached the clinic.

Dax and Bull did their best to hold Billy steady as the wagon took the rutted trail to town. Low moans broke through his lips several times, but his eyes never fluttered.

The streets were quiet, not an odd occurrence in late evening. The glow of lantern lights shone out the clinic windows, indicating at least one of the doctors was present. Two of the windows were broken, the front stoop a little askew. Taking a closer look around, Dax noted several buildings showed damage.

Rachel and Shining Star stood by the side of the wagon while the men lifted Billy from the wagon. Hurrying inside, Rachel found Clay McCord upstairs, alerting him to the reason for their presence.

Tad and Bull carried the stretcher inside, holding it still while Dax and Doc McCord transferred Billy to the examination table. His gaze scanning the injuries, the doctor began cutting off what was left of Billy's clothes.

"This from the earthquake?"

"He was trying to get Shining Star's son out of her house when the roof collapsed," Dax answered. "Appears the town got hit, too."

"Strongest shakes we've had since the tremblers started. Bull, get me that bottle on the counter and a couple of the cloth strips next to it. Has he woken up at all since you found him?"

"No," Bull answered, a catch in his throat.

Using the liquid from the bottle to clean the injuries, he picked up the supplies needed to suture the deepest wounds. "Wish I hadn't sent Georgie home. We had several people within a couple hours after the quake hit, then it quieted down. I thought there was no need for her stand around. Where'd Rachel go?"

"She's waiting out front with Shining Star. I'll get her." Bull returned a moment later, Rachel on his heels. Rolling up her sleeves, she went right to work.

The two worked well together, Rachel seeming to read Clay's mind. Halfway through, Billy stirred, one arm lifting before dropping back to the bed.

Rachel bent down close to his ear. "Billy?" When he didn't respond, she tried again. "Billy, can you hear me?"

A soft moan sounded before his eyes fluttered opened to slits. "Rachel?"

"That's right. You're at the clinic."

Blinking, he tried to focus on her face. "Why?"

"We'll explain it all when you're feeling a little better. Right now, you need to rest."

"Shining Star?"

"She's fine. So is the baby. You saved him, Billy."

Closing his eyes, he drifted back to sleep.

Dax got rooms at the St. James for those who'd ridden into town. All except Shining Star. She'd refused to leave the clinic. Doc McCord allowed her to sleep in the room adjacent to Billy. Before leaving, Bull gathered what she'd need for Spirit Bear from Suzanne Barnett.

They were up early the following morning. After breakfast, Rachel walked to the clinic with food for Shining Star while Dax, Bull, and Tad went to the jail. Gabe, Shane, and Cole were already inside, sipping coffee.

"Gabe."

"Dax, what brings you to town?" After the men shook hands, Bull and Tad took seats against one wall while Dax explained.

"Glad to hear Billy's going to be all right. He's a good young man. Did Dom Lucero come by your place, Dax?"

"He did. Told me one of his ranch hands went missing. Has he been found?"

"No, and neither have the others. I sent a couple men up into the mountains to check with those living in abandoned cabins and caves. They didn't find anything useful." Gabe massaged the back of his neck, strain etched on his face. "Four people missing, and we've found nothing to help us find out what happened."

"Has a connection between any of them been established?" Bull asked.

"You couldn't find four people more dissimilar than Amos, Winslow, Rose Keenan, and Charley. From what we've learned, the four never met each other."

The men shifted toward the door when it burst open. A haggard looking Ruby Walsh, the owner of the Grand Palace, gripped the doorframe.

"One of my girls walked to McCall's for supper, Gabe. She never returned."

Standing, Shane cupped her elbow, guiding her to his chair. "Sit down, Miss Ruby. Do you want some coffee?"

Waving him off, fear darkened her eyes. An emotion few would associate with Ruby. "Ada left to have supper at McCall's."

"Alone?" Gabe asked.

"Yes. She goes there several times a week for her meals. When she didn't return, I thought maybe something happened when the quake hit. I spoke with Betts McCall." Her worried gaze shot to Gabe. "She never went into the restaurant. Nor did she go to the boardinghouse to eat. All her clothes are still in her room, including the little jewelry she owns."

"Did any of the girls see her after she left for supper?" Dax leaned forward, his thoughts the same as the others.

Pulling a handkerchief from a pocket, she fidgeted with the edges. "No."

Standing, she shoved the chair aside, pacing a few feet away before whirling around to face the men. "I'd wager the Palace that Ada has been taken."

Chapter Eighteen

MacLaren Ranch

Two days had passed since the earthquake struck their property. The damage had been ten-fold of the others.

One mare had been running around the corral when the first, strong jolt shook the ground. She'd been unable to gain her balance, tumbling forward, fracturing both knees.

Grabbing his rifle from the house, Bram had put her down. Remorse at losing her lasted seconds before he had to face the devastation around him.

The four men had sat down for supper when the first tremors shifted the floor in the kitchen. A pot toppled over, spilling what remained of the stew onto the stove and adjoining counter. Pictures dropped from nails, a small table in the living room crashed to the floor, breaking one of its legs. None of them had waited to see the damage upstairs.

Staring at their untouched meals while waiting until the tremors stopped, they raced outside. Bram and Thane headed to the corrals while Kev and Vince ran to the barn. To their amazement, the only true damage was to the loft. The support columns had cracked under the weight of hay and the shaking earth. The platform lay in pieces, the stacks of hay strewn across the ground.

Tools had fallen from hooks. Several buckets were turned on their sides, the contents scattered around the large space. Thankfully, there were no horses in the stalls, all having been turned out before supper.

"It could've been much worse, Kev."

Not answering, the older of the Lathan brothers continued to survey the damage, noting what they'd need to rebuild the loft. It would set them back a few days from their normal chores, but Vince was right. They could've lost the entire barn.

After burying the mare, the four cleared out debris from the barn, Bram making a list of the supplies needed to rebuild the loft. By mid-morning, he and Thane were on the trail to Splendor. Bram knew Dax had planned for them to drive the herd to Fort Connall that morning, but there was nothing he could do. His ranch came first before riding to the Pelletier place.

They stopped several times to remove fallen trees from the trail. The quake's destruction was evident the entire way to town. Entering Frontier Street, the brothers reined up.

People scurried about, tossing large shards of glass and broken timber into wagons. Shop owners swept the boardwalk outside their stores while other men nailed boards where windows had once been.

"We should go straight to the jail." Bram rode down the street, avoiding the scattered debris. "Gabe will know if anyone needs our help."

Gabe wasn't in the jail, nor were any of the other deputies. Returning to their horses, they scanned the street.

"Are you looking for Gabe?" Bernie Griggs, the Western Union clerk and postmaster, bustled toward them. Keeping his distance from the horses, he bounced on the balls of his feet, hands flaying in the air. "He's not in the jail."

"Do you know where he is?"

"He and the deputies are searching for one of Ruby's ladies. She went missing last night. That makes five people. Gabe's got to find the no good scallywag taking them."

"Any idea where we'd find him?" Bram's mouth twisted.

Bernie shook his head, his words clipped. "Might be over at the Palace, but don't know for sure. Well, I'd best get back to the telegraph office."

Watching as he rushed away, Bram released a deep sigh. "Guess we should head over to the Palace, see if we can join the search."

Leaving their horses outside the jail, they walked the short distance to the Palace, stopping at the sight of a wagon and horses outside the clinic. Recognizing them as belonging to Dax and Bull, Bram changed directions. There was no reason they should be there unless someone was injured.

Pushing open the door, he glanced toward the closed examination room door before his gaze landed on Shining

Star. On the floor next to her, Spirit Bear slept in a basket. She looked to be dozing.

The door to the room opened, Doc McCord emerging with Dax.

"Bram." Dax held out his hand.

"What happened?"

"Billy was injured when the quake hit the ranch. He tried to get the baby out of Shining Star's house, but the roof collapsed. It's a miracle they both survived."

"Selina?" Bram asked before he could stop himself.

Brow lifting, a corner of Dax's mouth curved upward. "She's fine, as is everyone else. They're at the ranch cleaning up and making repairs. Hope those darn quakes have worn themselves out."

Thane moved beside his brother. "How's Billy doing?"

"Looks worse than he is," Doc McCord answered. "Dax should be able to take him home later today." He looked across the room at Shining Star. "I wonder if she and the baby have eaten."

"Rachel and Bull took them to the boardinghouse for breakfast, and she left a bit ago to bring food back from McCall's. Bull's seeing how the search for Ada is going."

"Isn't that five people, Dax?"

"Sure is, without any idea who took them or where they might be held."

"Assuming they're still alive." Bram had a hard time believing all five had been spared whatever the kidnapper had planned. "What are your plans for driving the herd north?"

Dax glanced over his shoulder at the room where Billy slept. "He insists on going."

"I doubt he'll be healed enough for at least a week," McCord added.

Bram rubbed the back of his neck, lips pursed. "We have five days to meet the deadline, Dax. What do you want to do?"

"We can't put it off any longer than the day after tomorrow. If Billy isn't ready, I'll send someone else. Any one of several ranch hands would be able to go."

Bram nodded, considering the idea of mentioning Selina. Her skills might not be at their peak, but she'd be able to keep up with the men.

"We've got Bull, Thane, Travis, Tad, and me. Do you need to add someone if Billy isn't ready?" Bram asked.

Rubbing his stubbled jaw, Dax considered the options. "Maybe not. With the newest quake, I could use the men at the ranch."

"You know Selina will want to replace Billy."

Dax's jaw clenched. "She isn't going."

Thane shuffled uneasily next to Bram. He'd already expressed his opinion to his brother. Selina's experience on short cattle drives, and with this set of horses, wouldn't hold them back.

The door of the clinic burst open, two men, faces browned and leathered, rushed inside. In the arms of one of them was a woman.

"You the doc?" The tallest of the two stopped in front of Clay. "We found her off the trail. She's alive, but not by much."

Even with her face caked in dirt, dress torn and filthy, Dax recognized her. "It's Rose Keenan. She's one of the missing women."

Gabe stood outside the examination room where Doc McCord and Rachel tended to Rose. Dax was beside the sheriff, waiting for answers from a woman who hadn't regained consciousness.

They gained little from the two cowboys who'd found her. The best they could provide was the location. Off the trail southwest of town. The description told them nothing.

She had nothing with her except the clothes on her back, which had been torn beyond repair. From what they'd seen, she had cuts and scrapes on her hands, legs, and face. She hadn't been carrying a coat or blanket, nothing to protect her from the cold spring night. The look of her scuffed shoes indicated she'd been walking for quite a while before collapsing.

"You sure you want to offer those men a job, Dax? Maybe I should have one of the deputies check the posters at the jail before you send them to the ranch." Gabe thought of the two men who'd brought Rose to the clinic. "It won't take long."

"Not necessary. Bram, Thane, and Tad have already left for the ranch. The two ranch hands are with them. Bull and I will follow later today with Rachel and Shining Star. We'll be keeping watch on them until we're certain they're nothing more than ranch hands."

Gabe understood, even if he didn't like it. "I'll send word if we learn anything you'd want to know about them."

The examination room door creaked open, Rachel resting against the jamb. Her eyes held none of the usual light Dax expected. Walking to her, he drew his wife into his arms.

"Rose still hasn't woken up." Her voice broke, arms tightening around Dax. "Clay couldn't find any reason why she's been out so long. We haven't been able to get any water or food into her. She'll die if we can't..." A sob burst from her.

Lifting her into his arms, Dax strode to a nearby chair and sat down. Cradling her in his lap, he stroked her hair. He could count on one hand the times Rachel had cried. It didn't worry him. She was bone tired after almost losing Billy and Shining Star's baby. Her friend, Rose, now fought for her life.

Dax leaned back in the chair, rubbing a hand up and down Rachel's back as the sobs subsided. If Rose died, not only would Rachel lose a good friend, the woman would take what she knew about the kidnapper to her grave.

Bull sat next to him as Rachel straightened in Dax's arms. "Three men and two women have disappeared. How do you think Rose got away?"

Shifting, Rachel moved to the chair on the other side of her husband, swiping at the moisture on her face. Bull's question made her think of the four others, wondering about their fate.

Dax took Rachel's hand, rubbing his thumb over her palm. "Whoever took them must've had his attention somewhere else, allowing her to sneak away. It wasn't planned."

Bull nodded. "No coat, gloves, blanket. She must've dashed off, running for her life."

"That would explain the cuts on her body and face. Rose ran out of fear."

Rubbing his chin, Bull cast a look at the examination room door. "The woman has a lot of guts. If I find the man who took her, it won't end well for him."

Dax understood. He and most every man for miles felt the same.

Gabe stood near the room where Rose lay, hearing every word the men spoke. He knew they wouldn't kill in cold blood, but they might take their time getting the kidnapper to jail.

"Why don't you head back to the jail, Gabe. I'll let you know when she wakes up."

He'd been so caught up in the conversation a few feet away, he hadn't noticed Clay emerge from the examination room. Turning, Gabe looked past the doctor to the bed. Rose rested in the same position as when the cowboys had brought her to the clinic.

"Might do that, Doc." Gabe's head turned when the door opened. Francesca, Christina, and one of the clinic nurses, Georgina, rushed inside.

Francesca walked straight to Gabe. "Is it true? Has Rose been found?"

"Yes, but she hasn't gained consciousness since being brought into the clinic."

"So you know nothing about who took her?"

"Not yet." Gabe rubbed the back of his neck. "As soon as Doc says it's all right, I'll be questioning her."

Francesca shot a look at Christina and Georgina before nodding. "I'd like to be there."

"As a friend or her lawyer?"

"Both."

"All right, but understand, I'll be asking the questions."

A corner of Francesca's mouth tilted upward. "I'll agree to that."

Gabe sighed, knowing whatever Rose could tell them wouldn't be easy for anyone.

Chapter Nineteen

Bram checked his saddle's cinch one more time. Satisfied, he took in the men around him. Bull, Travis, Thane, Tad, and Billy waited near the corral holding the horses.

It had been two days since they'd left the clinic. One since Billy had returned to the ranch, determined to be a part of the drive to Fort Connall. Neither Dax nor Doc McCord had tried to talk him out of it.

As one of the ranch's two foremen, Bull would lead the drive. Bram couldn't ask for a better man. He'd stayed with Billy at the clinic until the doctor gave his approval to leave. Bull had driven the wagon while Shining Star and her baby sat in the back with Billy.

After taking time to visit with his family, he'd met with Dax, Luke, Rachel, and several others, relaying information about Rose.

She'd woken a few hours after Dax and Rachel had left for the ranch. Gabe and Francesca had been called, waiting for McCord's permission to ask questions. Their disappointment had been acute when they learned she didn't remember anything.

Rose recalled getting ready for her shift at the boardinghouse, and stepping outside. From that moment until waking in the clinic, her memory failed. Nothing about who took her, others he may have kidnapped, or her escape.

Doc McCord reassured them Rose had a good chance of recalling the missing time. It could take days, maybe weeks, but the odds were good.

Francesca and Georgina had moved her back to the St. James, where Rose shared a room with Amelia. The three, plus Carrie Galloway, set up a schedule to check on her until Rose felt well enough to return to her job at the boardinghouse.

"You boys ready to roll out?" Bull reined his horse in a circle, making eye contact with each of the five men. "I'll take point. Travis and Bram, you're on left and right swing. Thane and Billy, you'll take left and right flank. Tad, you're taking drag. You'll switch around with Thane and Billy."

The sun's first rays lit the eastern sky, signaling for Travis to open the corral gate. Taking their positions, the men used coiled ropes to drive the horses past the main house before turning left to take the trail north.

Lydia, holding Joshua's hand, stood next to Shining Star, Spirit Bear asleep in the basket at their feet. Studying the young mother, Lydia saw worry crease her face. Shining Star might not have accepted her feelings for Billy, but her love for the young man was obvious to anyone who bothered to look.

"They'll be fine. The trip to Fort Connall and back won't take long. Bull has made it several times."

Hands clasped together, Shining Star swallowed the fear she wanted no one to see. "Yes. They will return."

Her words were stronger than how she felt. After losing the Blackfoot brave she loved, she couldn't think of losing Billy. He'd become her rock, the one person she could count on to protect her and her son.

Lydia let go of Joshua's hand, watching him wave at his father before Bull rode out of sight. "Do you plan to tell him how you feel?"

Shining Star's mouth dropped open before she closed it. "Feel?"

"Does Billy know you love him?"

Her beautiful, caramel-colored skin deepened, lips drawing into a thin line. How did Lydia know of her love for him when she'd accepted it only weeks earlier?

"It is not my place to speak of it."

"Don't you think he deserves to know?" Lydia persisted.

Shining Star's attention landed on Billy just as the bend in the trail forced him from her sight. "I have said nothing of my feelings."

Lydia understood. She and Bull had danced around their love for months before he'd admitted how he felt.

"Would it be a surprise if Billy loved you?"

Instead of answering, she bent down, picking up the basket holding her son. "I will prepare breakfast now."

Stepping off Lydia's porch, her shoulders squared. Walking to the house Dax and Luke had given her to use, a small smile tilted her lips. After months of worrying about her future, Shining Star thought perhaps she and her son might have a place at Redemption's Edge.

Selina stood at her bedroom window, staring at the retreating horses surrounded by six men. Frustration, anger, and jealousy warred within her. All attempts to ignore the building resentment at not being included had failed.

Her mind and heart told her she should be with them. Months had gone by with her working six or seven hours a day with Travis and Billy, preparing herself for a journey such as this one. Bram and Thane's arrival had been a huge benefit for Dax and Luke. Not so much for her.

With the increased contracts, Travis had spent most of his time with the MacLarens while she watched from the fence line. Billy had included her when possible, the time amounting to a couple hours a day at most.

She tried to hate Bram and Thane for ruining her dream. It had been a pointless waste of energy. Bram's skills were the equal of Travis's. Thane's the equal of Billy's. The four worked as if they'd always been together. She'd become a hindrance in the race to fulfill the Army contracts.

"Selina, breakfast is ready." Rachel's voice had her moving, her focus still on the plans formed over the last few days. Dressed in the pants and shirt she wore for working with the horses, she rushed downstairs.

"What are your plans today?" Rachel handed her a plate filled with eggs and bacon before taking a seat next to her.

"With the men gone, there's no one to work with me and the remaining wild horses. My time would be better spent repairing broken bridles and saddles. I heard you will be riding back to town to see how Rose is doing."

"Yes. Ginny and I will both be heading into town after breakfast. We may stay the night."

Selina wanted to cheer. The longer the women were gone, the better for her own plans.

Nibbling at a perfectly fried slice of bacon, she picked up her cup of coffee. "Does Doc McCord truly believe her memory will return?"

"Clay does think, given time and rest, she'll recall what happened."

"I hope he's right. Perhaps Rose will be the key to finding the other four. Are Gabe and his deputies still searching?"

Taking her plate to the sink, Rachel washed and set it aside. "On a much smaller scale than before. He doesn't know where else to look."

"What about the cave where you found us?" Selina still recalled their escape from the Crow renegades.

Five children, Lydia being the oldest, had stayed for days in a damp, inhospitable cave not far from Redemption's Edge. Billy had gone for help when Lydia took ill. Nothing the children did helped her recover.

Dax, Luke, Bull, and a few other men had found them. It had turned out to be the best day of all their lives.

"There are hundreds of caves in those mountains. Gabe has sent deputies, but the area is so vast, they couldn't have covered it all."

"I don't understand how someone could take five people and leave no tracks or clues. Surely the men would've fought."

"And the women." Rachel thought of Rose. Her quiet nature hid a strong woman with determination and grit. "Dax believes the kidnapper used chloroform. Maybe knocked the victims out before dragging them to a wagon, or tossing them over the back of a horse. He said it's easy to cover up tracks using branches."

"I should get to the barn." Washing her plate, Selina turned to face Rachel. "Are you sure it's safe for you and Ginny to ride into town? Anything could happen."

Rachel patted her arm. "It's been the same since I moved to the ranch after marrying Dax. To be safe, one of the ranch hands is going with us. It's getting late. I'd better check on the boys. Lydia and Margaret will watch the children while we're gone." Walking toward the hall, Rachel stopped. "Is there anything you need from town?"

"Nothing, thanks."

Thinking of her plans, Selina bit her lower lip, beginning to feel the first pangs of doubt. Her words to Rachel played in her mind. *Anything could happen.*

Shaking off the warning, she dashed upstairs for her gloves, coat, and hat. Selina would work in the barn until

Rachel and Ginny left. When out of sight, she'd fetch Honey.

Selina pushed her mare in an attempt to catch up with the group heading to Fort Connall. Her plan was simple. The first day, she'd stay far enough away so they wouldn't spot her. If they saw her too soon, Bull would send her back.

By noon of the second day, she'd let her presence be known. Bull would be angry, tempted to send a man back to the ranch with her. Once he'd cooled down, he'd realize continuing north would be the best decision. Her punishment could wait until they returned to Redemption's Edge.

The herd came into sight mid-afternoon. From her location about a hundred yards away, she could see each man's location. Her gaze landed on Bram. If she weren't mistaken, he had taken the right swing position, close to the front of the herd.

As she watched, he reined his horse around, waving to Tad, who rode drag, at the back. In less than a minute, the two had changed places.

Signaling Honey to move into the cover of the trees, she relaxed in the saddle, taking in the scenery around her. Selina had never been this far north of the ranch. The stories Bull and the others told after returning from each trip to the Blackfoot village fascinated her.

Reaching behind her, Selina pulled a pouch of jerky from the saddlebag. Tearing off a bite, she again thought of the Blackfoot village, wondering if they'd ride anywhere near it. From the map she'd found on Dax's desk, Fort Connall had been built a good distance northeast of the village.

Billy had told her a great deal about the tribe, how they'd been in the same location for years. He'd made it clear how rare it was for the people not to relocate several times a year. Running Bear had made the decision to send smaller groups east in the spring to follow the buffalo, rather than the entire village packing their tipis to make the long journey.

Billy believed it had a great deal to do with crossing land inhabited by the Crow tribe and the Blackfoot location close to Wildfire Creek. The area was rich with game, the valley protected from the worst of the storms.

Before she realized how far they'd traveled, or noticed the sun dropping behind the western ridge, Bull signaled for the men to stop. Selina glanced around, and sighed. She'd be making camp in the brush unless she could locate a better spot.

Waiting to confirm the men had found their camp for the night, she slid to the ground. It took little time to remove the saddlebags, heavy coat, and bedroll before releasing the saddle and bridle. Honey walked a few feet away to a small pond before grazing on a broad expanse of grass.

Too close to the herd to make a fire, she satisfied herself with biscuits and sliced roast beef. Slipping into her coat, Selina found the perfect place for her bedroll and stretched out. Within minutes, she'd fallen asleep, a smug grin tugging at her lips.

Chapter Twenty

"The way Selina's snoring, nothing's going to wake her." Bull's jaw clenched as he stared down at the most stubborn woman he'd ever known. The fact she was his sister-in-law made it worse. "I'll take her horse. Are you able to carry her on your gelding?"

Bram scoffed at the idea he couldn't take the load. "The lass won't be a problem. Not until she wakes up. Maybe it would be best to tie her over Honey's saddle."

A laugh burst from Bull's throat before he could contain it. Both men stilled, hoping the sound hadn't woken Selina.

They'd spotted her following them soon after Bram changed spots with Tad. He hadn't believed his eyes. Then she'd moved from the cover of the trees' shade and into the sun. Cursing, he called for Thane to take drag while he rode to the front to give Bull the bad news.

Not wanting to spare a man to take her home, they'd decided to let her make camp before fetching her. There'd be time to tear a strip off her once they returned to the ranch.

Tucking the blanket around her, Bram slipped his arms under her legs and back, then stood. Walking to his horse, he handed her to Bull before mounting. Reaching down, he took her from Bull, settling her on his lap. Swinging up on Abe, Bull grasped Honey's reins in one hand, his horse's in the other.

"Has she stirred?"

Bram shook his head at Bull's question. "The lass is still out. I'm hoping she'll stay asleep until tomorrow morning."

"Doubtful, though it won't matter. I just want to be watching when she does wake up." Bull led them out of the trees toward the herd.

Bram stared down at the woman in his arms, a strange sensation flowing through him. He'd been fighting his attraction to Selina since first discovering he liked her. Much more than he'd thought possible.

Buried behind the men's clothes and touchy nature was a beautiful, smart woman. Lifting a hand, he swept strands of golden brown hair off her face, hesitating a moment to admire the splattering of freckles across her nose.

Unable to stop, he caressed a path along her jaw, his fingers slowing as they continued partway down the slim column of her neck. Feeling her stir, he withdrew his hand. Bram couldn't imagine the storm he'd create if she woke up to discover him touching her face.

Riding into their camp, Bram waited until Bull placed Selina's bedroll near the fire before taking her into his arms. "Didn't wake at all, did she?"

"Nae. The lass didn't stir at all." Dismounting, he couldn't pull his attention away from Selina. Holding her had affected him more than he wanted to admit.

Bram didn't want to feel any attraction to the feisty beauty. He'd heard about how she'd once been a sweet, congenial girl. From what he'd observed, she still was within the Pelletier family.

Not long after making the decision to become a wrangler, her entire personality had shifted. As Bull described it, instead of the pleasant young woman he'd come to know, her attitude changed to surly and disagreeable. A few weeks of training with Travis had given her the idea she was as good as any man on the ranch.

Grabbing his tin cup, Bram filled it with coffee, walking to where Selina slept. Lowering himself onto the ground a few feet away, he listened to her even breathing.

Watching her, Bram found himself wondering how the girl she'd been had changed into a cantankerous young woman. Something must've happened for her to make such a drastic transition. But what?

"Looking at her now, you'd never suspect what a disagreeable gal we'll be dealing with in the morning." Bull crouched down next to Bram, sipping from his own cup. "Never saw the change coming. Near as Lydia and I can recall, it happened about the time of her eighteenth birthday. Right after, Selina asked Dax about working with Travis and Billy. When she traded her dresses for men's clothes, we lost her. At least that's the way Lydia describes it."

"Did you ever ask her about it?"

"Lydia did, but Selina told her nothing happened. She doesn't believe her, but we can't make the gal talk."

Finishing the last decent swallow of the cooling brew, Bram tossed the grounds behind him. When Selina stirred, both men stilled. Barely breathing, they waited as she turned to her side, let out a low moan, then settled into her bedroll.

Glancing at each other, Bull and Bram exchanged relieved looks. Neither were ready to deal with Selina and her disregard for Dax's clear order. She'd rant, but wouldn't be able to hide from whatever punishment would be dealt out once they returned to the ranch.

"I want you to stay close to her, Bram."

Bull's order stunned him. "The lass won't be happy about me being her keeper."

"She doesn't have a say in it. I need a man who'll have the strength to deal with her dark moods and the complaining that's coming." Standing, Bull tossed the last of his coffee in the dirt a few feet away. "Tad, Travis, and Thane will let her get away with her griping. Billy is too close to her, like brother and sister. You're the best one to deal with Selina. Where you ride, she goes, too. I'd prefer you take right swing."

Bull being the trail boss, Bram wouldn't argue. Instead, he trudged the short distance to his bedroll. Stretching out on top, he clasped his hands behind his head, thinking of the days ahead.

What had started out as a pleasant trail drive to Fort Connall had turned into an annoying complication. He should've expected Selina to follow. They all knew she'd been set on going with them. Bram didn't object to her joining the men, but it was Dax's decision, and he'd been firm in her staying behind.

Staring up at an ink black sky blanketed with glimmering stars, he closed his eyes. Within minutes, he drifted off into a fitful sleep.

Blinking several times, Selina stretched both arms above her head, letting out a contented groan. She hadn't expected to sleep through the night without a fire to warm her. A crackling sound had her brows furrowing.

Leaning up on her elbows, she caught sight of a roaring fire before spotting several men watching her. Men she knew quite well.

"What the…" Sitting up, she flung the bedroll aside and jumped up, mouth dropping open.

"Morning, sunshine." A few feet away, Bram fought to contain a chuckle at her confusion. "Sleep well?"

Hands fisted, she stomped toward him. "What am I doing here?"

"An excellent question, Selina." Bull, his features rigid in anger, walked toward her. "What *are* you doing out here? Dax was clear. You were to stay at the ranch."

She'd known her brother-in-law for years, and had never seen him so irate. For the first time since making the decision to follow them, Selina began to doubt her actions.

"I wanted to be included."

"After being told you wouldn't be going?" Scrubbing a hand down his face, Bull shook his head. "There aren't enough men for me to send one back with you, and there isn't a chance you're riding back alone."

Excitement burst in her chest. "So I can go?"

"Only because you've given me no choice. You'll be with us on this drive." Bull let out a frustrated breath, his gaze boring into hers. "Enjoy it, because it may be the last one you'll ever be a part of."

The excitement she'd felt vanished in a wave of regret. Why couldn't she control her impulses? Ever since realizing her dream was to work with horses, she'd pushed, cajoled, and aggravated everyone around her. Her latest action may have ruined all she'd worked so hard to achieve.

"I'm sorry, Bull." Unable to meet Bram's searching gaze, she stared at the ground, feeling a warm flush creep up her cheeks.

Settling fisted hands on his hips, Bull pursed his lips in a tight line. "Why do you always have to fight everyone? There are reasons Dax and Luke make decisions, and they aren't to make you mad. He had plans for you back at the ranch."

"Plans?"

"Doubt you'll hear about them after this stunt. Listen good, Selina. You'll be riding alongside Bram the rest of the trip. The two of you won't be more than ten feet apart...day and night." He raised his hand when she opened her mouth to protest. "Don't think about arguing with me. Bram is no more happy about this than you, but someone has to keep a bead on you. Do you understand what I'm saying?"

Straightening her back, she lifted her chin. "I'm not daft, Bull. Yes, I understand."

"Don't know about you not being daft, Selina. What you did, defying Dax, doesn't make you appear too smart."

Resisting the urge to turn her back on him, saddle Honey, and ride out, she set aside her broken pride and nodded. "You're right. It was dumb and irresponsible."

"Rachel is probably going out of her mind with worry. Wouldn't surprise me if they believe the kidnapper got you. Dax might have men out searching for you. Men who can't afford to be taken away from their work."

Whatever remorse she felt doubled at his words. Of course they'd believe she'd been taken.

"Maybe I should ride back now."

"No!" Bull and Bram shouted in unison.

"I can be at the ranch well before sunset."

"You aren't listening, lass." Bram shot a look at Bull, who nodded. "Get breakfast and be ready to ride out. We're leaving as soon as you're ready."

"I won't be long."

Billy came toward her, holding out a biscuit with bacon between the halves. "Here, Selina. I'll get you what's left of the coffee."

Bram watched as she chowed down the food, following it with the coffee Billy gave her. His chest constricted at the misery on her face.

Turning away, he checked the cinch, bridle, and reins, a ritual he did before any ride. Bram knew he shouldn't, but with nothing more to do, he tacked up Honey while Selena rolled up her bedding.

"I can take care of my own horse."

"I know you can, lass." Bram nodded toward the others. "We're holding up the lads. Secure your bedroll and mount up. We've a lot of ground to cover."

Sucking in a ragged breath, Selina stifled a curse which would horrify her sister. She'd been stupid to follow the men.

"Bram, wait." Rushing to catch up, she clasped her hands together. "How did you find me?"

Glancing past her, he reached out, touching her arm. "We spotted you yesterday afternoon."

Eyes wide, her mouth dropped open. "How? I was so careful."

"Aye, you were. When I changed spots with Tad, movement in the trees caught my attention. The shirt you have on..." His gaze moved to the red flannel shirt. "It's easy to spot in the sunlight."

Looking down, she felt a wave of embarrassment. Not the first that morning.

"But I stayed in the shade of the trees."

"Not all the time. I wouldn't have seen you if you had."

"So you watched me, knew where I bedded down?" Her voice had softened, the initial frustration disappearing. "I should've been more careful."

"You shouldn't have been there at all, lass. Truth is, I'm glad you wore the red shirt. You've no idea of the dangers being alone on the trail."

"I didn't see anyone."

A grim smile tightened his mouth. "What about the small group of Blackfoot who followed us for a couple hours?"

Crossing her arms, Selina's jaw clenched. "You are not serious. I would've seen them."

"Did you?"

Dropping her arms, she couldn't miss the truth on his face. "Two hours?"

"Aye. Bull recognized Swift Bear. They exchanged signals before the group rode off."

"Do you think they saw me?"

"Lass, *you* were who they were following."

Chapter Twenty-One

Riding alongside Bram wasn't a hardship. Selina loved watching him ride, even if she did have to sneak glances at him from several feet away.

Over the years, she'd seen hundreds of men sit a horse, admiring less than a couple dozen, and most of those worked at Redemption's Edge. From the first time she'd seen Bram and Thane ride onto the ranch, she'd known they were special. It didn't take long before she realized they were hired for the job she'd worked hard to get.

Staying several feet to his right, she studied every move. How he flicked his rope or the way he reined Bullet when a horse tried to move outside the herd. His moves were fluid, the result of a rider comfortable in the saddle.

Selina wondered how she looked when riding Honey, was even more curious as to how Bram saw her. Not that his opinion mattered, she reminded herself.

"Do you see what Tad is doing, lass?"

His question startled her, forcing Selina's attention from his strong legs and arms to his face. The twitch of his lips signaled he'd caught her staring.

She made a weak attempt at glancing over her shoulder. "Um...no. What's he doing?"

"He's riding drag, which isn't too bad with our smaller herd of horses. With steers, the dust they kick up can almost blind the rider in the back."

Placing one hand on the cantle, she supported herself while looking to the back. "He's riding back and forth."

"Aye. The lad's making sure the horses know who's the boss."

"Does it work?"

Bram chuckled, his eyes crinkling at the corners. "Depends on the skill of the rider, size of the herd, and the terrain. Bull has known Tad a long time. He trusts him riding drag."

Selina continued to glance over her shoulder as the group continued north. Billy rode right flank, which put him between them and Tad.

"Billy looks tired."

"Aye. The lad refused to be left behind." Snorting out a laugh, he shot a look at Selina. "The same as you, lass."

"I shouldn't have followed. Lydia, Rachel, and Dax are going to be so worried about me."

"The entire ranch will be thinking the worst." Kicking Bullet, he cut off a gelding and two mares wandering away from the herd. Returning, he reined his horse around. "Bull thinks there's a telegraph at the fort. If so, he'll let Dax know you're with us."

Which meant Bernie Griggs would be riding out to the ranch, taking him away from his office in town. The consequences of her leaving continued to grow. After this, she'd be lucky if Dax allowed her to work with the horses ever again.

"Look." Bram pointed to a flock of geese. "They're flying north for the summer. They'll return south again when the weather changes."

Shielding her eyes from the mid-morning sun, she stared into a cloudless, blue sky. "They're beautiful. How many do you think there are?"

Bram turned his attention away from the herd and back to the sky. "I see four flights. My guess is there are at least a hundred geese in each flight."

Her eyes narrowed. "Four hundred birds?"

"Aye. I've seen as many as six flights close together. Minutes later, several more appear. There are tens of thousands that make the trip north each year."

She lowered her head to look at him, head tilting in confusion. "I thought you'd arrived in Montana at Christmas. Do you see them in California?"

A grin brightened his features. "Aye, lass. I've seen them fly over our ranch many times."

Biting her lower lip, Selena struggled with the question she'd wanted to ask since he and Thane had arrived in Splendor. Until today, there'd never been a good time.

"Tell me about your ranch."

Gaze scanning the herd, he didn't answer right away. He missed his family, his friends in town. Over the months since arriving, he'd tried not to think of them, choosing to focus on the new ranch, and his work for the Pelletiers.

"Bram?"

Staring at the rope in his hand, he looped it over the saddlehorn before wiping moisture from his brows.

"My family bought the land years ago. Father and my three uncles made the decision, although we all had a say about selling our farm outside Philadelphia and joining a wagon train west. No one had seen the land until we rode over the last mountain." He paused, remembering his first reaction to the spectacular sight before them. "I've never seen anything so beautiful." *Until now*, he thought, looking at her.

"Dax said your family grew it into a thriving cattle ranch."

"As large as Redemption's Edge," Bram added. "Over the years, we added horse breeding and training."

"Why'd you leave?"

Rubbing his stubbled jaw, Bram considered his answer. Leaving had been a long time coming. His mind went back to the final discussion he and Thane had with their family. Even his cousin and her husband had ridden in from their ranch north of Conviction to give their opinion.

There'd been anger, tears, frustration, and finally, resignation from those who didn't understand Bram's desire to leave. There were days he still didn't comprehend what spurred him to walk away from a life he knew and loved. Sometimes, you had to follow your heart, and not your head.

"It's not an interesting story, lass."

She turned a wan smile in his direction. "I do believe we have plenty of time. I'd love to hear the story."

From working together at the ranch, he knew Selina wouldn't let this go. A dog with a bone is how Bull described her. With several hours ahead of them, Bram figured he might as well spend the time explaining his past, and maybe learning more about her.

"My family is large. Everyone owns a piece of the Circle M. In return, we all have specific jobs based on our skills and interests. The women take part the same as the men. Most wanted to work with the cattle. A few of us decided to grow the horse breeding business."

He burst ahead, cutting off a few wayward horses before returning to ride beside Selina. "Sean, one of my cousins, wanted to attend Highland Society's Veterinary School in Edinburgh."

"In Scotland?" The awe in her voice had Bram grinning.

"It is, lass. The family saved the money for him to attend. He returned not long before Thane and I left." He swallowed. Of all his cousins, he missed Sean the most. They'd been exchanging letters, the same as when Sean had studied in Scotland for all those years.

"With his return, the ranch had another person who loved working with the horses."

Selina shifted in the saddle to look at Bram. "A veterinarian and horse breeder. He must be busy."

"Aye." Bram thought of the expression on Sean's face the day he and Thane rode out. If he wasn't mistaken, there'd been a tear running down his cousin's cheek. The image always triggered a pang of guilt.

"Thane and I talked for over a year about expanding beyond northern California. Sean helped us research. He sent letters and telegrams to ranchers and politicians in several states. Not bragging, but the MacLaren name had spread beyond the borders of California. Long discussions with our family ended in us choosing between Colorado and Montana. When Griff MacKenzie received an invitation to meet with Francesca, we decided to ride out with him."

Nodding, her brows scrunched together. "Why the two of you?"

Shrugging, he changed the reins from one hand to the other. "We were ready to go. Plus, neither of us were married."

"Everyone else was?"

Something flickered in Bram's eyes before disappearing. "Aye. All those my age and older are married. Except for Sean. The lad is shy. He'd rather work with the animals than attend any of the town socials." His mouth twisted into a grin.

She watched him for several seconds, deciding whether or not to ask one other question. Knowing she might not get another chance, Selina made her decision, hoping her voice didn't waver.

"Have you ever been close?"

Cocking his head, one brow lifted. "Close?"

"To asking a woman to marry you."

Ready to answer, he caught movement at the front of the herd. Bull had turned in his saddle, motioning for Bram to join him.

"Stay here." When Selina began to follow, he reined around to face her. "You need to stay on swing while I talk with Bull." He waited until she gave a sharp nod.

Riding forward, he glanced at the hills on both sides of the valley, seeing nothing to alarm him. So far, it had been an easy drive. Almost too easy.

"We have company," Bull said when Bram reached him. "On the east is a group of what appear to be Crow."

"I didn't see them."

"They dropped behind the hill right after I signaled you." Bull looked behind him at Billy. The younger man's hand rested on the butt of his revolver. Their gazes met, confirming what he suspected. Billy had seen the Crow party and expected a fight.

Glancing over his shoulder, Bram saw the same as Bull. Billy prepared himself for an attack.

"What do you want to do?"

Bull held up his hand, indicating to the others he meant to stop. "Hadn't planned to, but we'll break for lunch. We circle up the horses before telling the others about the Crow."

Bram shot a sideways look at the hill, catching a glimpse of the group Bull had seen. "It'd be best if the Crow don't know we've spotted them."

"Agreed." Holding his hand in the air, he made a circling motion, letting the others know to tighten up the herd.

Riding back to Selina, Bram's features were grim. "Don't react, but there's a small party of Crow following us." Face paling, he saw her hands, then her shoulders shake. "What's wrong?"

"Are you sure they're Crow?" Her voice trembled.

"Bull's the one who spotted them. He's certain they're Crow."

Giving a slow nod, she forced her racing heart to slow. "He would know."

Bram didn't know what she meant, but vowed to find out once they reached the fort. "Stay on your horse and keep the herd in a tight circle."

"They want the horses." Selina's fingers grasped the reins. "If they're part of the renegade band, killing whites to get what they want won't matter."

"If they're not?"

Selina lifted one shoulder in a shrug. "Then we might have a chance of getting the herd to Fort Connall."

The answer came a moment later.

Chapter Twenty-Two

A blood curdling scream, unlike anything Bram had ever heard, pierced the air. Pounding hoofs and war shouts followed as the band of Crow raced down the hill toward the herd.

Bram counted seven, all holding rifles instead of the bows and arrows he expected. Launching himself at Selina, they toppled to the ground, his body covering hers. He'd made the move almost an instant too late as bullets hit the ground around them. Rolling off her, he put pressure on her back to keep her down.

"Stay where you are." His tone brooked no argument.

"I can shoot as well as you." Drawing the gun from the holster around her waist, she rested her elbows on the ground, aimed, and fired. Although the shot didn't kill her target, the bullet caught the Crow's shoulder, tumbling him off his pony.

Aiming his six-shooter, Bram squeezed the trigger. Missing, he aimed and fired again, this time hitting his target in the thigh. Rifle and gunshots continued, along with the shouts of the attacking Crow.

Looking to his right, he was relieved to see Thane firing, then reloading. When he looked to his left, his heart stopped. Bull lay on the ground, unmoving.

Without thinking it through, Bram stood. Bending at the waist, he hurried toward his friend, firing as he ran.

Covering Bull's body with his, Bram got off two more shots, one finding its mark.

He counted four braves still riding, watched one of them topple backward off his horse. The horses had scattered the instant the Crow attacked. Without any protection nearby, his friends lay flat on the ground, firing as targets appeared.

Carefully checking Bull, he cringed at the sight of blood pooling beneath his shoulder. The hairs on the back of his neck prickled as the war hoots started again.

Raising his revolver, he shifted in the direction of the shouts. What he saw stunned him.

Riding down the hill from the west was another group of braves. At first, he thought they were another party of Crow. Then he spotted the leader.

Swift Bear, thighs gripping the sides of his pony, rifle against his shoulder, fired. With him were at least ten Blackfoot riders, all with bows or rifles. Between Swift Bear and the men from Redemption's Edge, they were able to turn back the Crow, forcing them back over the eastern hills.

Finding the wound in Bull's shoulder, he ripped a strip from his shirt, pressing it against the hole. Lifting him enough to see his back, Bram let out a relieved sigh. The bullet had gone straight through.

"Did you see Swift Bear? They're driving the Crow away." Billy's joy vanished when he stared down to see Bull. Dropping to his knees, his worried gaze met Bram's. "How is he?"

"The bullet went straight through. Can you get the whiskey out of my saddlebag?"

Jumping up, Billy ran to where Selina still held her six-shooter. "Where is Bram's horse?"

"Why?"

"Have you seen Bullet or not?"

"Over there." She pointed toward the base of the eastern hill. Bullet and Honey were together.

Running toward them, Billy whistled, thankful both horses came toward him. Reaching into one saddlebag, he cursed under his breath when he didn't find the whiskey. He had better luck with the second saddlebag. Grabbing the bottle, he started to hurry away, then stopped.

"Keep the horses close."

"What happened?" Then she looked to where Bram knelt beside a prone body. "Is that Bull?"

"Yeah." Before he could explain about the shoulder wound or the whiskey, she took off at a run.

By the time he caught up, Selina was on her knees, taking over pressing the rag against where the bullet entered. Handing Bram the whiskey, Billy turned in a circle. Thane, Tad, and Travis worked alongside the Blackfoot to round up the horses.

"I'm going to help them, Bram."

"Selina, will you be all right for a few minutes?"

Opening the bottle, she poured whiskey on the entry point of the wound. With Bram's help, they lifted him so she could do the same on the exit spot. Gently lowering him back to the ground, she again pressed the strip of fabric against the wound.

"Yes, but he needs a doctor."

"There should be one at Fort Connall."

Billy searched for his horse, spotting Swift Bear riding toward him, rifle lifted into the air in celebration. Stopping inches away, the Blackfoot warrior met his friend's expectant gaze.

"Billy Zales."

"Swift Bear. Thank you for coming to our rescue."

"The Crow raid close to our village. Running Bear sent us to protect you." Swift Bear tipped his head toward the eastern hill. "They have gone." His attention moved to the man on the ground. "Bull Mason?"

"He took a bullet to the shoulder."

Swinging his right leg over his pony's neck, Swift Bear slid to the ground. It took little time for him to understand the nature of the wound.

"You are going to Fort Connall with your horses?"

Billy removed his hat, running a hand through his hair. "Yes, but with Bull shot..." His voice trailed off.

"We will take Bull Mason to our village."

Bram moved next to Billy. "What?"

"This is Swift Bear. He is Shining Star's brother. He's offered to take Bull to their village."

"Can they treat a gunshot wound?" Bram asked.

Swift Bear's impassive expression didn't change. "My people have good medicine. Bull Mason will be well when you return from the fort."

Bram shifted toward Billy, a brow lifted. "What are your thoughts, lad?"

"The Blackfoot medicine is probably as good or better than what we'll find at the fort. I trust Swift Bear's word."

"So do I." Travis had ridden up, choosing to stay atop his horse. "The village is closer than the fort."

Bram scrubbed a hand down his face before looking at Swift Bear. "We would appreciate your help."

The warrior's lips tilted up the tiniest bit. "It is a good decision."

The rest of the drive to the fort was uneventful. No more sightings of the Crow renegades. Travis took Bull's place as the trail boss, locating himself at point. There were other changes in positions, with Selina riding right flank behind Bram.

Three hours passed before their destination came into view. The fort was larger than Selina anticipated. Their approach signaled the guards to open the gates, allowing the men and horses to enter. After the last horse entered the corral, a trooper moved quickly to close the gate.

"We made it." Selina dismounted, unable to contain a grin as she joined Bram and the others.

Without thought, he placed an arm across her shoulders. "That we did, lass."

"I'll see if the colonel is in his office." Travis started up the steps, stopping when the door opened. Colonel Miles

McArthur stepped outside, his gaze moving over the wranglers. Stopping for moment on Selina, his attention lingered several seconds before joining Travis.

"Colonel McArthur. You may not recall me, but—"

"I remember you, Mr. Dixon, although I was expecting Bull Mason." His focus shifted once again to Selina.

"We ran into that pesky band of Crow renegades. Bull was shot."

Moving past the group to the corral, he studied the horses. "Have you taken him to the infirmary?"

"Funny thing, Colonel. A party of Blackfoot showed up and ran the Crow off. The Blackfoot chief, Running Bear, is friends with the Pelletiers. His son, Swift Bear, took Bull back to their village for treatment."

McArthur swiveled to look at Travis. "The Blackfoot are taking care of him? Is that wise?"

"They have medicines we know little about," Travis said. "Nothing against your doc or ours, but I can testify most of their treatments are as good or better than what we can get from infirmaries and clinics."

Without responding, he strode straight to Selina. "I'm Colonel Miles McArthur."

To Bram's disgust, she grinned at the officer. "Miss Selina Rinehart, Colonel."

His gaze moved over the men's pants and shirt she wore, keeping his opinion to himself. "You rode in with the wranglers?"

"Why, yes. In fact, I am one of the wranglers."

"One of the best you'll ever see." Bram moved close to Selina's side. Close enough to send a message to the colonel. He wasn't surprised to see the man's gaze narrow on him.

"Mr. Dixon. The quartermaster has approved the delivery and will provide the agreed upon dining room." With that, he returned to his office.

"We're having supper with the colonel, Bram. Isn't it exciting?"

His mouth twisted as he saw the anticipation on her face. "Aye, exciting."

An unexpected surge of jealousy wound its way around his heart, becoming a lump in his belly. He couldn't recall ever experiencing the loathsome sensation. Bram had never loved a woman, hadn't expected to find someone in Montana. If the ache in his chest was an indication, he could be in trouble.

"What will we do until supper?"

Selina's question drew him from thoughts of her and his growing feelings. "We'll move our gear to where we bunk down. There's usually a store in every fort. We can look for it, if you'd like." She didn't miss the lack of enthusiasm in his voice.

"Are you all right, Bram?"

"Couldn't be better, lass."

"One of the soldiers is going to show us where to bunk down." Billy stopped beside them, his saddlebags over his shoulder.

Following the private and Billy, Bram didn't check to see if Selina was behind them. Bram knew he was being discourteous...and ornery. The realization he found her a desirable woman instead of a pain in his arse didn't sit well with him.

On the rare occasions when he thought of the type of woman he'd want to marry, he pictured someone more refined, slender, who looked fetching in a dress. A woman who other men stared at when she passed by.

Men did stare at Selina, but it wasn't because they found her fetching. Her choice of men's clothes, heavy boots, and cowboy hat turned heads all the time. She was a curiosity, especially when people knew Lydia, Rachel, and Ginny. Women who worked alongside men while showing off a softer side. He didn't even know if Selina had a softer side.

Reaching their quarters, the private pointed out the bunks before showing Selina to a small room off to the side. From her expression, Bram was certain she'd prefer staying with the men.

Shaking his head, he tossed his saddlebags on one of the cots, lowering himself onto the edge. Scrubbing both hands down his face, he felt as if he were falling down a deep, dark hole.

Of all the women in the world, why did he desire one as vexing and stubborn as Selina Rinehart?

Chapter Twenty-Three

Supper dragged on, Bram's anger rising as Selina gifted McArthur with a series of smiles. When she laughed, the crystal clear sound reached him at the other end of the table.

Upon entering over an hour earlier, McArthur's aide had pointed to their places around a long, rectangular table. The colonel sat at the head, Selina seated on one side of him, Travis on the other. Everyone else took places down each side. Bram ended up as far away from Selina as possible. He had no doubt the exile had been McArthur's doing.

The food was well above average, much better than trail fare. The whiskey flowed fast and often. Most times, Bram couldn't hear the conversation between the three at the other end, which he took as a blessing. It wouldn't do to show the jealousy bubbling in his gut.

Finishing his dessert and coffee, Bram pushed back his chair and stood. "Thank you, Colonel, for your generous hospitality. Unfortunately, we'll be rising early to ride back, so I'll be turning in."

When the others stood, McArthur held out his hand to Selina. Bram didn't wait to see or hear what was said, preferring fresh air and a walk before bunking down.

Taking the steps to the ground, he rubbed a hand at the back of his neck while looking around. Sucking in a deep breath, he began a path around the inside perimeter of the fort. He found it hard to focus on anything except his jumbled feelings for Selina.

Bram didn't understand the woman's effect on him, the unease mixed with excitement, which sputtered through him when Selina was near. He'd never experienced anything close to the odd sensations she created.

"Hey, Bram. Wait up." Thane jogged toward him, rubbing his belly. "Best meal we've had in a while."

"You mean since leaving our ranch."

"True. You are as good as any woman in the kitchen, older brother." A sharp shove to his shoulder had Thane laughing. "What happened back there?"

"Needed air."

"It was more than getting outside. As fast as you left, seemed you were running away." There was no malice in Thane's voice.

Bram stopped, facing his brother. "Have you ever seen me run from anything, lad?"

"No, but you've never been interested in a woman."

Jaw ticking, Bram tilted his head back, staring at a sky so similar to what they'd expect at Circle M. These were the times he missed his family, joking with his cousins, playing with the growing number of children running around the ranch. Tearing his gaze back to Thane, he gave a sharp shake of his head.

"I've no interest in any woman."

Thane barked out a robust laugh. "Not from what I've seen. You've a strong interest in Selina, and she feels the same about you."

"The lass doesn't have feelings for any man."

"You've never been able to lie, Bram. Selina couldn't stop sneaking looks at you during supper."

"The lass couldn't take her eyes off McArthur, not me."

"She was being polite."

Bram choked out a snort. "The lass isn't polite, Thane. She tolerates people."

Reaching the corral, they watched the horses a minute before doubling back to retrace their steps. "The two of you got along well on the drive."

Bram thought of her questions about his family, the Circle M, and his reasons for leaving. He'd told her all except the true motive for seeking a change. A reason he'd shared with no one. Not even Thane.

"Bull told me to stick with her. I couldn't ignore the lass."

Thane's lips twitched at the ridiculous statement. He knew his brother well, and he'd bet his horse Bram held an interest in Selina.

Opening the door to their quarters, the rumbling sounds of snoring reached their ears. They'd never had to adjust to sharing space with other men, except when traveling in steerage across the Atlantic. It had been years ago. Bram had been eight, and Thane three. The entire MacLaren clan had huddled together, all the children considering it an exciting adventure.

They'd still been young during their short stay in Philadelphia. When the uncles planned the houses at Circle M, everyone had their own room.

Walking past the cots, Bram looked toward the closed door to Selina's room. He could see a soft gleam under the door, indicating an oil lamp still burned.

For a brief moment, he considered knocking, telling himself it was to check on her. In truth, he wanted to see her once more before claiming his own bed. Lifting his hand, he hesitated.

Glancing to his right, Bram flinched. Thane sat on the edge of his cot, watching, one side of his mouth lifted in a knowing grin.

Dropping his hand, Bram stalked back to his bed, removed his boots, and slid under the blanket. Cursing at himself for being a fool, he forced his eyes closed. Tomorrow would be soon enough to check on Selina, and sort out the feelings making him appear an eejit.

Selina tamped down the urge to open her door and peer into the bunk room. Bram had stomped out of the colonel's quarters after dessert, and hadn't returned to the small building where they slept before everyone turned in.

She'd kept her lamp burning, hoping he'd knock. The idea was ridiculous. Bram wanted nothing to do with her other than fulfilling his commitment to Dax...and now to Bull.

Her eyes stung at the thought of her sister's husband. Without doubt, Bull was one of the best men she'd ever known. And he loved Lydia with his entire heart. She prayed allowing Swift Bear to take him to the Blackfoot village had been the right decision. Not that she'd had a say.

Knowing they'd learn Bull's progress soon, her thoughts returned to Bram. She didn't understand how any man could control so much of her waking time. From sunup to sundown, he was inside her head. Selina realized she wanted him to stay there.

Extinguishing the lamp, she pulled the blanket under her chin. Closing her eyes, a smile formed. She fell asleep with an image of Bram breaking a mustang.

It was a fitful sleep. Tossing and turning, she woke often. Something bothered her, but she couldn't decide what.

Selina didn't believe it was concern over the punishment awaiting her at the ranch. Perhaps not knowing Bull's condition troubled her. Or the potential of another Crow raid on their trip home.

Not until she thought of Bram did the reason for her unease become clear. When they returned to the ranch, he and Thane would return to their ranch until the Army gave them another contract.

Rachel had told her Dax and Luke were waiting for word on several proposals, not expecting responses until sometime after the horses were delivered to Fort Connall.

Meaning, she might not see him again for weeks.

An odd emptiness claimed her when she closed her eyes. Selina couldn't imagine so much time passing without seeing him. Not long ago, she'd considered him the enemy, recoiling when he'd arrive each morning.

How her feelings had changed.

Dusters did little against the torrential rain pounding down on the group of riders. Fort Connall lay several hours behind them, too far to ride back for shelter. The Blackfoot village stood a few hours southwest from their current position. They had no choice but to continue on.

Selina swiped water from her face before sending another furtive glance toward Bram. He'd been polite, though distant, when they'd prepared to ride out of the fort not long after sunrise. His silence on the trail hurt. Nothing she said or did gained the slightest response.

Travis had declined the colonel's invitation for the group to join him for breakfast. Undeterred, the colonel's cook had provided each of them several biscuits, bacon, and slices of sweet bread. They'd finished the provisions long ago. All Selina wanted now was a hot cup of coffee to warm her hands.

"How are you doing?"

Startling, she hadn't noticed Travis rein up beside her. "Wet. Cold. Ready for shelter. Otherwise, I'm fine." Noticing Bram ride over to join them, she stiffened.

Offering her a curt nod, Bram turned toward Travis. "We should find shelter. The storm is getting worse, not better."

"You're right. Our best chance is on the other side of Wildfire Creek."

"Assuming we can cross it." Bram changed his attention to Selina. "Are you warm enough, lass?"

"Yes."

Eyes narrowed, he studied her. The blue lips and red-rimmed eyes belied her lie. "Do you want me to ride ahead, Travis?"

"Both of us will go. Billy and Tad know the way to the creek. Selina and Thane will be safe following them. I'll let everyone know what we're doing." Travis raised his hand, signaling for the riders to circle up.

It took seconds for him to explain and take the trail west. Bram took one last glance at Selina before turning his attention to locating shelter.

Billy took the lead while Tad rode behind Selina and Thane, both vigilant for impending danger. Following the same trail as Bram and Travis, they entered the forest. The trees provided a small amount of protection from the downpour, but not the cold.

Selina's duster felt heavy, her hat and gloves almost soaked through from the intense rain. As the wind picked up, nothing except shelter would help them from becoming chilled clear through.

After slogging through the deep mud, they welcomed the harder ground of the forest trail. They'd lost sight of

Bram and Travis almost as soon as the two broke away from the group.

A wave of panic coursed through her at his absence. With Bram close, she felt safe, protected from whatever danger may come their way. The Crow attack had illustrated how little she knew about life away from the ranch. Selina might come across as haughty and able to handle anything, but the reality was she'd been somewhat sheltered.

The Pelletiers and their ranch hands always put the safety of the women and children first. The men faced any danger directly. Proficient with rifles, scatterguns, and revolvers, the women were still relegated to the protection of the house during a crisis.

Carefully slipping a hand inside her duster, Selina confirmed the presence of her Colt six-shooter. If the Crow attacked again, she'd be ready to eliminate the threat.

The sound of hoofs pounding on the soaked ground had the group glancing around. Seeing the men go for their weapons, she did the same, wishing she'd brought her shotgun. On instinct, the four drew closer, creating a small amount of protection. The wait was the worse.

Bram crashed through the brush, Travis right behind him. Facing four weapons pointed at their chests, the two raised their hands.

"Sorry." Billy slid his rifle back into its scabbard.

"Our fault, lad. We found shelter not too far ahead." Bram's gaze landed on Selina as she slid her Colt away.

“We were eager to get back to you.” His attention never wavered from her as he spoke the words. “Ready?”

A tingling sensation started in the area around her heart, settling as a smile formed on his face. She matched it with a grin of her own.

“Ready.”

Chapter Twenty-Four

Splendor

"I'm sorry, Sheriff. The man who took me never removed his mask. And all the other victims had sacks over their heads. He took mine off when he brought in the last victim. A woman." Rose's features reflected the misery she felt. "I remember being in an old shack, but not its location."

Setting a hand on her trembling shoulder, Gabe's voice softened. "It's all right, Miss Keenan. You've given me more than I expected. Are you certain he was alone? Didn't have partners?"

"I can't be sure, but as far as I could tell, there was just him."

Gabe nodded, knowing he was missing something, but not what. "You're sure there were four other people in the shack?"

"Yes. He took us to the privy separately, so it was clear there were four. We weren't allowed to talk to each other. One of the men tried, and was beaten. No one chanced it after that."

Gabe leaned forward, clasping his hands together on bent knees. They were in the room in the St. James she shared with Amelia Newhart. She'd moved back there a few days earlier after Doc McCord gave his approval.

"Did you know when he left the shack?"

"No. I do remember thinking the room where he held us had to be quite small. We couldn't stretch out our legs without touching one of the other prisoners. We did have to pass through another room before going outside."

"What about using the facilities?"

"As I mentioned, he took us outside one person at a time, twice each day. We still wore the hoods, and our hands were tied, but he removed the ropes around my ankles."

Rubbing his jaw, Gabe's brows drew together. "Could you tell if he was tall or short?"

"I'm pretty certain he was taller than me. He has broad hands and a raspy voice." Her eyes widened. "I almost forgot. He has long hair."

"How do you know?"

"He'd guide us outside with a hand on our shoulder. One time, I slipped. When my hands sought something to steady myself, I grabbed long hair. Real long. The kind most men pull back in a queue."

"What did he do?"

"Yelped, grabbed my wrist to rip my hand away. He didn't hit me, if that's what you mean."

Gabe sat up, glancing at the few notes he'd taken. "Tell me once more how you escaped."

Slipping a strand of hair behind her ear, Rose pursed her lips, casting a glance at the deputy leaning against the wall. He was new to Splendor, serious looking, and quiet. And quite handsome.

"It wasn't planned. He took me outside to use the privy. I could tell by the number of steps we were almost there when I heard an explosion. Or what I thought was an explosion. I heard his footsteps moving away from me, and well…I didn't think. I just ran."

"You removed the sack over your head?"

"Not at first, but after tripping, I tore it off and continued running." Rose licked her lips, glancing down at her clasped hands.

"Your hands were tied in front?"

"Yes. It was dark, so even though the sack was gone, it was hard to see. I didn't want to take time to remove the straps. Thinking back, I should've. If I had, I'd never have tripped and rolled down the hill."

"You're lucky you didn't crack your head open."

Rose lifted her head to look at the deputy. It was the first time he'd spoken. "You're right. It was a miracle I didn't kill myself. My understanding is that's where those two cowboys found me."

"They weren't real specific about the location. As you said, it was dark. They tried to find the spot with a couple deputies, but couldn't pick out the location. Do you think you would have better luck?" Gabe was running out of options.

Rose shook her head. "I'm sorry, but I wouldn't have any idea where to look."

"Do you know how he got you out of town, and to the shack?" This came from Cole.

Balling her hands into fists, her lips pressed into a thin line "No. I was getting ready for my job at the boardinghouse. The last thing I remember is reaching for my coat. When I woke up, there was a sack over my head, and my hands and ankles were bound. It was terrifying."

Gabe shot a look at Cole, knowing they were thinking the same. Rose Keenan had been through a great ordeal. No matter the obstacles, they'd find the shack, the hostages, and the man who'd abducted them.

"He's gone. I'm sure of it." Ada Hockson continued to work the bindings on her wrists, ignoring the suffocating sack over her head.

Silence greeted her, as it had since one of the prisoners had escaped days before. Ada believed it was a woman their captor had taken outside, but she'd never returned. The man who'd kidnapped the people in the shack had stormed back inside. His rants continued for long minutes, the sound of objects being tossed around increasing her anxiety.

"Is anyone in here with me?" Ada knew there were. Heavy breathing, coughing, and the occasional grinding of boots against the wood floor assured her she wasn't alone.

Sagging back against the rough wood wall, she renewed her efforts to release the bindings, with less enthusiasm this time. Ada knew they'd been left alone. She'd heard the stomping hooves of a horse as it moved away from the shack. Her head snapped up when someone spoke.

"What are you doing over there?" A man's voice, rusty with lack of use, surprised her. There was a formality to the tone, as was common from those of the upper classes back east.

"Trying to get out of the darned bindings on my wrists. I'm close."

"Won't do you no good." This came from her right. The voice sounded young, uncultured. What she'd expect from one of the local cowboys who frequented Ruby's Palace. "Mine are too tight. I've been trying since I got here."

"I'm not giving up. We don't know who he is or what he plans for us." Ada hesitated a moment, considering her next words. "If I can scoot across the room, maybe one of you could try to release my bonds. We'd have everyone free within minutes."

"I'll give it a try." A new voice, older, low, and rough. "Don't know where you are, but I'm against the north wall. I've been here the longest, and will do what's needed to get away."

"All right." She began scooting forward. "I can follow your voice."

"I'm right here, missy. Don't think more than a couple feet." As he spoke, he could hear her moving toward him until her shoes touched his.

Ada let out a relieved breath. "I'm holding out my hands. Can you feel them?"

"Yep." Already loosened from her efforts, he didn't have to work long to free the bindings.

Shoving them off, she grabbed the edges of the hood, whipping it off her face. "Oh my. I can see all three of you."

Grabbing the wrists of the man who'd freed her, Ada released his bindings. Once he'd torn off the hood, he moved to one of the other men while she loosened the rope of the third man. It took little time for them to free their ankles and stand.

"I know you," Ada said. "You came into the Palace with Silas Jenks."

"Yes, ma'am. I'm Amos Henderson. I used to own the Wild Rose."

"I'm Ada Hockson." She looked at the other two men.

"Charley Jones. I work for Dom Lucero."

The third man took his time, brushing dirt from his suit coat. After a while, he raised his head. "Carson Winslow, from Boston."

Charley bent down, scooping up his hat from a corner. "Nice to meet y'all, but I think we should get out of here. I'll go first." He reached for his gun, only to realize it wasn't there. "Damn. Wonder where he put my gun."

"Doesn't matter, Charley." Amos looked at the others. "We'll worry about our personal stuff later."

Opening the door, Charley glanced around before stepping outside. Moving forward, he continued to check their surroundings before waving for the rest of them to join him.

"Which way?" Ada turned in a circle, seeing nothing except the privy and a stack of firewood.

"Straight down. We have to get off this mountain before dark," Amos answered.

Charley adjusted his hat, jaw set. "Or that madman returns."

"Over there." Ada pointed to a deer trail a dozen yards away. "Will that work?"

A smile crept across Amos's face. "That'll do fine. Let's go."

"Wait." Carson made his first contribution to the conversation. "What about food or water?"

Charley shook his head. "Won't need it if we get down this mountain soon. We should come out close to Wildfire Creek. From there, we can find our way to one of the ranches."

"Let's go. You go first, Charley. Ada, you go right after, then Carter. I'll go last." Amos motioned for them to hurry.

The narrow trail, used by deer, elk, and few other critters, was perfect for the four. Wide enough to pass, but still secluded with the cover of bushes and trees.

Charley moved as fast as possible while keeping watch for threats. Bears and mountain lions were often out in the daylight, while wolves preferred the cover of darkness to attack their prey. Without a rifle, they were vulnerable to attack.

Their footfalls were all they could hear as they made their way down. The trail wound to the left then right, but continued toward the creek below. Charley had grown up on a small ranch west of Splendor, knew the area as well as anyone. He knew how easy it was for people to disappear. Entire families had wandered off and never been seen again.

A grunt behind him had Charley stopping. Amos's curse and Ada's yelp preceded Carson rolling toward him. The man tripped on a root or rock, crashing to the ground. Momentum propelled him forward, crashing into the brush until he came to rest against a tree trunk a few feet from Charley. Kneeling down, he checked Carson for injuries.

"You all right?"

A low growl sounded from the easterner's throat. "Hell no, I'm not all right." Taking Charley's hand, Carson stood, swaying. Getting his balance, he winced. "Tripped on a rock."

"You all right to keep going?"

"Fine. I'll stay behind you. In case I trip again."

Charley didn't respond. He suspected the man wasn't used to being relegated to a place near the back of anything. With four people, the two spots that mattered were first and last. Charley looked at Ada and Amos.

"You folks ready?"

"Yep," Amos answered. "We need to get to the creek before it gets dark."

A hundred yards down the trail, Charley heard the unmistakable sound of a moving wagon. Creaking wheels, leather slapping on the back of a horse or oxen alerted him their captor wasn't far away. Turning, he held up a hand for quiet. Squatting, he motioned for the others to do the same.

Listening, Charley could no longer hear the wagon. The forest was eerily quiet. No birds. Not even the rustling of leaves.

Rising, his eyes widened. Not a hundred feet away, a man holding a rifle searched the area around him. Heart pounding, his gaze latched onto the others, praying they understood the need to be quiet and stay down. In the dwindling light, they'd be hard to spot.

Holding their breath, the four waited. Minutes felt like an hour to those whose lives were in danger. Then Charley heard it. The wagon began to move away from them.

Rising a second time, he watched as the man steered the horse up the mountain. He was heading to the shack, which meant he didn't know they'd gotten away.

Moving to the others, he kept his voice low.

"We have to get out of here. He'll discover we're gone in a few minutes. We have to be far away by then." As each gave a curt nod, he stood, and bending at his waist, began to run.

Minutes passed, giving the impression they'd gotten away. The crack of a rifle changed their mind. With a cry of pain, Carson dropped to the ground.

Chapter Twenty-Five

Cash Coulter and Beau Davis, two of Gabe's deputies, stood, dropping the fishing poles they'd been holding. Until then, it had been a peaceful afternoon. So much so, and even in the growing darkness, neither were ready to ride back to Splendor.

Neither had missed the crack of a rifle. Reaching for the six-shooters around their waists, they visually scoured the area on the other side of Wildfire Creek. Nodding at each other, Cash led the way across the fast flowing water, then up the hill.

A scream reached them at the same time a rifle fired again. Increasing their pace, the deputies put a few yards between them.

"Run!" The yell from up the hill had them scrambling.

"It came from our left." The words left Beau's mouth seconds before three people crashed toward them. "It's Amos."

"And Charley Jones." Cash's gaze narrowed on the woman. "Must be Ada Hockson with them."

"Beau. Cash." Amos stopped between them.

"Get down," Charley yelled. "He's still behind us."

"Keep going to the creek and get to the other side. Cash and I will keep the shooter away for as long as possible." Beau didn't look behind him as he and Cash continued up the hill.

They'd slowed their pace, moving from one hiding spot to another while watching for the gunman. As quickly as the shots started, they stopped, the forest around them quieting.

Cash narrowed his gaze, looking for any movement ahead of them. "What do you want to do?"

Beau rubbed his stubbled jaw. "I *want* to go after the kidnapper. What we *should* do is protect the people who got away."

"You're right." Taking one last look up the hill, Cash retraced their path to the creek, Beau right behind him. "Where are they?"

Forging across the creek while keeping watch behind them, they scooped up their fishing poles and rushed to their horses. Several feet away, Amos, Charley, and Ada brushed leaves and dirt from their clothes and hair.

Cash wasted no time with pleasantries. "Who kidnapped you?"

Charley spoke first. "We don't know. He kept sacks over our heads. We didn't eat all at one time. He removed the sack from one of us, let us eat, then replaced the hood before moving to the next person. You gotta know, he shot one of us. He's still up on the hill."

Beau and Cash exchanged a look. "Carson Winslow?" Cash asked.

"That's the name he gave." Charley shook his head. "Don't know if he's alive or dead."

"Did you get a good look at him while you were escaping?" Beau asked.

Amos shook his head. "When he started shooting, I was too busy running."

"Same with me, Deputy." Ada ran fingers through her tousled hair that hadn't seen a brush in days. "I was too scared to turn and look."

"Charley?"

"Didn't get a good look, Beau. Wish I had. I'd go back and make sure he never again abducted anyone."

Grabbing canteens from his horse and Beau's, Cash handed them to the three. "We didn't bring any food, but we're not too far from the Pelletier ranch."

Amos's mouth twisted. "How are we going to get five people to their place using two horses?"

Beau shifted toward Charley. "Do you know how to get there?"

"Sure do."

"Ada will ride with you on my horse. Amos, you'll take Cash's horse. When you get to the ranch, send a couple men back with our horses." Beau glanced at his good friend. "Cash and I will keep watch here in case the varmint who took you shows up."

"Hope he does. I want to see him hang for what he did to all of us." Ada fumed with anger. "Did another captive make it back to town? A woman, we think."

Cash nodded. "Rose Keenan made it down the mountain, then collapsed. A couple cowboys took her to the clinic. She couldn't tell us much. Not your location or anything about your abductor. She's still recovering."

Ada stared at the ground. "I know Rose. She works with Suzanne at the boardinghouse. Nice lady. Hope she'll be all right."

"Doc McCord thinks she'll be fine." Cash walked to his horse, handing the reins to Amos. Swinging into the saddle, he looked down at the deputy.

"We'll send men back right away, Cash."

"Appreciate it, Amos. And watch your back. We don't know where your abductor is now."

They waited until the horses were well away before turning to look up the mountain. Cash checked his rifle and six-shooter.

"Dead or alive, we can't leave Winslow up there."

Beau's mouth twisted into a feral grin. "I'm ready when you are."

Selina felt the warmth of a firm body at her back. It took several seconds to recall why she wasn't alone in her bedroll, and why it felt right.

Travis and Bram had shown them the thick cover of large bushes backed on two sides by wide expanses of boulders. The wind had slowed, even if the rain had continued a steady downpour.

After crawling under the cover of the branches, each had found a small space to curl up and wait. An hour passed, then two, the rain not letting up. Travis had found it impossible to start a fire, so they kept warm as best they could.

After four hours, Selina had felt her body shake, lips tremble. Pulling off her soaked gloves, she'd rubbed her hands together, blowing on them to relieve the icy cold.

Still shivering, she'd felt Bram come up next to her. "Get inside your bedroll, lass," he said, holding it open for her.

A few hours later, she'd woken with his muscled arm around her waist, his chest to her back. Even in his own bedroll, the heat of his body triggered tremors of desire in her stomach.

Shifting to create some distance, his arm tightened around her. Selina's heart pounded so fast she was certain the others in the shelter could hear it.

Others. She stiffened.

Selina forgot they weren't alone. Face heating, she tried again to move away from his embrace. Again, he wouldn't allow it.

"Settle down, lass. The rain is still pounding. We aren't going anywhere for a while."

"But the others—"

"Don't care we're keeping each other warm," he interrupted. They were so close, his warm breath fanned across her cheek.

Billy chuckled. "He's right, Selina. Go back to sleep. You're keeping the rest of us awake."

"Your turn, Tad." Travis touched Tad on the shoulder. "Though I doubt anyone will come after us during this storm."

Travis, Tad, Thane, and Billy had been given shifts as guards. Thane and Travis had gone first, neither spotting a threat.

"Only a fool would be out in this weather, Travis." Tad sat up, stretching his arms above his head. Standing, he gripped the rifle next to his bedroll. "Wish we had coffee. We've got the water."

Travis chuckled. "But not the fire."

"That's for darn sure," Tad replied, moving close to the front of the shelter.

Selina stayed within the warmth of Bram's arms, listening to the banter. Bram was right. Refusing his closeness would be foolish for more reasons than the heat he provided.

She found comfort in his arms, in the way he pulled her back against him. His presence sent tendrils of desire pulsing through her body, creating a throbbing need new to her. The sensations scared and thrilled Selina. She wanted nothing more than to remove the barriers between them. The knowledge frightened her.

Snuggling against him, she heard his strangled groan. "Are you all right, Bram?"

"I will be, once you settle down, lass."

She didn't know what he meant, but refused to cause him pain. Closing her eyes, Selina thought of Bram and how this might be as close as she'd ever get to the rugged cowboy.

Bram closed his eyes, cursing himself as a fool. He'd known being close to Selina would test his willpower. His desire for the beautiful young woman had grown during their trip, forcing him to accept he was falling in love.

Fighting his feelings had been a worthless use of energy. An image of Selina accompanied him into sleep. Waking, his thoughts were on her. Instead of thinking of the work ahead of him, his mind focused on one often cantankerous female whose smile melted his heart.

Lying beside her had been as much torture as pleasure. Bram found he craved the nearness, wished there were no barriers, even as he knew the bedrolls saved them from possible disaster.

He'd always thought of himself as a rational person, a man not swayed by a fetching female. Bram kept his emotions locked tight when it came to any woman. He found it impossible to rely on sheer will with Selina.

She broke down his barriers, creating a longing impossible to ignore. The problem was clear. Realizing he loved Selina, wanted her in his future, how did he convince the argumentative and independent woman to give them a chance?

When she woke again, she realized the rain had stopped, and Bram was no longer behind her. She immediately missed his warmth, the feel of his hard chest against her back.

Sitting up, her mouth dropped open. Everyone was gone, their bedrolls missing, the sun shining outside their shelter. Pulling on her boots, she stood, grabbing her bedroll before rushing through the opening.

Bram held the reins of her already saddled horse. Holding out his other hand, he took the bedroll, securing it with leather straps.

"Here." Thane held out a strip of jerky, along with a biscuit from the day before.

"Thanks." Her gaze landed on the streaming water, deep mud, and branches still dripping from the rain. It would be a long, slow ride to the Blackfoot village.

"We waited for the sun to dry some of the trail, lass. Travis decided it would take days. We'll leave when you're ready."

Chewing the last of her biscuit, she swallowed, wishing for coffee to wash it down. "I'm ready."

"You'll ride with me, lass." Bram walked away before she could formulate a response.

Her first instinct was to shout after him, insist she be the one to choose who'd ride beside her. Something stopped her. A desire so strong, she found it hard to protest as she once did.

Mounting, she made the rare decision to keep quiet. Selina had a great deal to think about, not the least was her strong attraction to Bram. Not a mere attraction, which confused her already muddled thoughts about the man.

Her feelings for him were so much more than a passing attraction. There were few men she admired. The Pelletiers, Bull, Travis, and Billy. The last not so much for his knowledge, but his steadfast devotion to the family who'd saved them, and his loyalty to Shining Star.

With a start, she realized the circle had increased to include Bram. Men she trusted without reservation were in the exclusive group.

Did she want him there? Did she trust him to the same degree as the others?

Selina didn't have to dwell on the answers. Without doubt, both questions were answered with a resounding *yes*.

Riding in silence toward the Blackfoot camp, she pondered her situation. Admitting to herself she not just admired Bram, but was falling in love with him, gave her small satisfaction. The true question was, did he feel the same about her?

Chapter Twenty-Six

Splendor

Shane Banderas finished breakfast at the boardinghouse, leaning back in his chair to stare outside. Several days had passed since Ada Hockson had disappeared, and they'd yet to find any trace of her.

The information from Rose Keenan had provided little. A man above average in height, with broad hands and long hair. The description could point toward at least fifty men in the area. A man Rose couldn't identify because she hadn't seen the kidnapper's face.

"More coffee, Shane?" Suzanne stood over him, a pot of coffee tipping toward his cup.

"No, I..." Pausing, he straightened in his chair when Angela entered the dining room. "Yes, more coffee would be good."

Turning to see who had caught his attention, a mischievous grin lit her face. "Nice woman. Sad how her fiancé is missing with the others."

Clearing his throat, Shane gave an almost imperceptible nod. "Yeah." Standing, he walked toward Angela. "If you aren't meeting anyone, you're welcome to sit with me."

Lifting her chin, she met his gaze. "If it isn't inconvenient."

He almost laughed at the formality. She'd changed a great deal since they'd been young and in love. When he'd been told she had died.

"I wouldn't have asked if it was."

Pulling out a chair, he couldn't help recalling how there'd never been money to treat Angela to a restaurant meal. They'd shared picnics in the woods, walks, and rode the horse his parents had owned. Anything where money wasn't involved. Her engagement to Carson Winslow turned her into a woman Shane no longer recognized.

"Is there any word on Carson?"

"Nothing yet." He waited while Suzanne filled Angela's cup with coffee. "You heard about Rose Keenan escaping?"

"Yes. My understanding is she doesn't remember much."

"Nothing useful. Are you hungry?"

"Not very." She blew across the top of her cup before taking a short sip.

Studying her more closely, he noticed the dark circles under her eyes. "When was the last time you slept?"

She continued to hold the cup in her hand, not answering at first. Setting it down, Angela leaned forward. "I'm not sleeping much or eating. I seem to have lost my appetite."

Lifting a hand, he motioned for Suzanne. "Please bring eggs and toast for Miss Baldwin."

"It isn't necessary, Shane." Her protest sounded weak.

Suzanne looked between the two before turning toward the kitchen. A minute later, she returned with a slice of fruit bread and butter.

"Start with this. There's plenty more in the kitchen. Just let me know." Suzanne cocked a brow at Shane before leaving the two alone.

"This wasn't necessary." Angela stared down at the plate before taking a small bite. "This is quite good. Does she make everything herself?"

"Suzanne or her cook." Shane waited as she picked at her food.

The tension between them was thick, the same as it had been since she and Carson arrived in town. How could it not be? He'd thought her dead. Instead, her life had continued while he'd suffered the pain of her loss.

His mind burned with questions. Why had her family lied to him? Where had she gone? How did she meet Winslow? Did she love him?

Shane had made up his mind not to ask. The answers would change nothing.

Crossing his arms, he relaxed back in the chair, his attention drawn outside. Frontier Street teamed with activity. Wagons loaded with supplies rolled through town while townsfolk filled the boardwalk. Life moved on as if five people hadn't been kidnapped.

Dropping his arms, Shane straightened. Cash and Beau rode past by the boardinghouse, followed by a wagon. Holding the lines was Amos Henderson. Standing, he sent a warning look at Angela.

"Stay here. I'll be right back."

"What is it?"

"Probably nothing." Rushing outside, Shane headed for the jail, his gaze locked on a woman in the back of the wagon. He was certain it was Ada Hockson, and she appeared to be tending to someone.

Reaching the wagon, he peered inside as Amos stopped outside the jail. His jaw clenched, recognizing Carson Winslow. "Is he alive?"

"Barely," Ada answered, pressing a blood-soaked cloth against the bullet wound.

"Best to head straight to the clinic, Amos. Cash and Beau will let Gabe know what happened." Shane wanted to hear the tale, also, but getting Winslow medical help took priority.

"Oh, no." Angela stood beside him, her face paling.

Shane pulled her away from the wagon, turning her to face him. "You were supposed to wait in the restaurant."

"Is he alive?"

"Yes. Come on. We'll meet the wagon at the clinic." Shane took her elbow, guiding her to the street behind the jail. "Go let the doctor know we have a man who's been shot. I'll help Amos carry him inside."

Gripping his arm, Angela searched Shane's face. "Do you think your doctor can save him?"

The worry for her fiancé tore at something deep in his chest. There'd been a day when Angela had cared about him as much. But those days were long in the past.

Hardening his heart and voice, Shane met her troubled gaze. "Our doctors are as good as any you'll find in Boston. Now, go inside." Setting her aside, he ran to the wagon, ignoring the woman he knew still watched him from the clinic steps.

By the time they'd set Winslow on the examination bed, Gabe had arrived. He went straight to Amos, gripping the shoulders of his friend.

"Are you all right?"

"Made it out of there, didn't I?' The voice was rough, but the smile on Amos's face told how much he appreciated Gabe's concern.

"All right. You all have to leave me alone with the patient." Clay McCord motioned for his nurse, Georgina Wise, to close the door behind them.

"When was the last time you ate, Amos?"

The older man nodded toward Ada, who sat with her head in her hands near the window. "The Pelletiers fed us and gave us lodging last night. I've got to get their wagon back to them."

"Don't worry about it now. I'll take care of it. Give me a moment to speak with Shane and we'll head to the jail. I want to hear the entire story."

Shane stood next to where Angela sat, back as rigid as the muscles in his face. He'd rather be anywhere except standing next to the woman he used to love, watching her whisper words of prayer for her wounded fiancé.

"Shane. I need to speak with you."

Breathing a sigh of relief at the interruption, he joined Gabe several feet away.

"How's Miss Baldwin doing?"

Glancing over his shoulder, Shane shrugged. He couldn't find it in him to care one way or another about how she felt. "Waiting for word about her fiancé."

"I'm taking Amos to the jail. Get word to me when Doc knows more about Winslow."

"Is there someone who can stay with Angela? I want to hear what Amos has to say."

Gabe studied him a moment, lifting a brow. "Angela, is it?"

Shane hadn't realized his mistake until it was too late. Now wasn't the time to explain. "Yes. She asked me to call her that." The lie tasted bitter, but the truth wouldn't go down any easier.

Although sensing a lie, Gabe didn't push. "If there's anyone at the jail, I'll send them over."

"I'd appreciate it." Retreating to retake his place next to Angela, he glanced down at her clasped hands.

Shane said nothing as he watched. Her features spoke of concern, not the anguish he'd expect from a man's fiancée. She showed a stoic silence, as if waiting for word about a long lost relative than a man she planned to marry.

A niggle of doubt wormed its way inside Shane before he shoved it away. What did he care if she didn't love her fiancé? A good number of people married for reasons other than love, the most common being money and social status.

Angela had grown up with neither. Her father had been a man who coveted both, not achieving either before Shane left town. Perhaps the marriage had more to do with fulfilling her father's dreams than her own.

His thoughts ended when the door to the examination room opened and Clay stepped out. Walking to them, he sat on the chair next to her.

"How is he, Doctor?"

"Not good. I understand you are Mr. Winslow's fiancée."

"Yes…"

"Then I'll be candid. The bullet did a great deal of internal damage. I'm afraid there is less than a fifty-fifty chance he'll survive."

Angela gasped, a hand covering her mouth. Shoulders slumping, she sucked in a slow breath. Instead of breaking down, she met Clay's compassionate gaze.

"When will you know more?"

"If he makes it through tonight, his chances of recovering will improve. Infection will be a possibility for several days, though. If that occurs, it will be a drastic setback. I'll do what I can, but you should consider thinking what you want to do if he doesn't make it."

Glancing away, she gave a slow nod before returning to face Clay. "You're right. I will send a telegraph to Carson's mother. The woman isn't in good health. It will devastate her if he doesn't survive."

"If you'd prefer to stay here, I'll send the telegraph." Shane didn't know why he'd offered.

Her eyes lit with gratitude. "You wouldn't mind?"

"Not at all. I need to go to the jail afterward. Will you be all right while I'm gone?"

"I'll ask Georgina to sit with her, Shane."

"Thank you, Doctor, but I don't want to occupy your nurse's time. I'll be all right waiting out here."

"We'll both be here, so Georgina sitting with you won't be a bother. Besides, she's from back east. I've been told she traveled to Boston several times." Clay offered a self-satisfied grin, believing he'd found a way to comfort Angela.

The reality was quite different. She'd disliked the eastern seaboard city since her first glimpse from the window of the private railroad car. The same as she'd abhorred her father for sending her there.

But that was a long time ago. Her path had been set, the pain of her past losses buried in the reality of an altered future. Now, through a series of astonishing events, Carson fought for his life, while the love from her past acted as if they'd never been close.

No one could be blamed except Angela. If she'd been stronger, less afraid.

If only she'd been the woman Shane deserved.

Chapter Twenty-Seven

Redemption's Edge

Selina worked alongside Rachel, Ginny, and Lydia in the kitchen, wearing an apron over a dress which hadn't left her closet in months. The blue cotton fabric with white flowers enhanced her green eyes, golden brown hair, and sun-brightened skin. She didn't care how it looked. What soured her mood had more to do with not being with Bram, Travis, Billy, and Thane...and the horses.

The group had arrived back at the ranch a few days earlier after finding Bull recovering at the Blackfoot village. It had been a blessing the rifle shot had gone straight through. The poultices the tribal women applied had avoided infection. When the group rode into the village, they'd been surprised to see Bull walking, ready to head home to his family.

Selina dreaded their return, unable to stop thinking about the punishment Dax and Luke had planned for her. Not long after arriving, they'd ordered her into the study. After stern comments about disappearing, they'd told her to stay away from the horses until they decided otherwise. It was the worst of punishments, but no less than she deserved. Since then, she'd spent her time cooking, working the garden, and doing all she could to be of service.

Rachel had insisted there be a celebration supper for Bull's quick recovery and return to the ranch. Hence the reason for the cotton dress barely covering scuffed brown boots.

Bull thought the fuss a ridiculous waste of time. He wanted to return to his job, get out with the herd, and prepare for a late spring roundup. Dax insisted he stay close to the house for a few more days before riding back out. A decision his wife, Lydia, applauded, and Bull cursed.

The sound of boots on the wood floor had Lydia dropping the spoon into the pot of stewing vegetables and hurrying to the dining room. Instead of Bull walking toward her, Bram stood at the edge of the living room, hat in his hands as he fingered the brim.

"I'm guessing you're wondering when supper will be ready," Lydia said in greeting.

A grin tipped one corner of his mouth. "Nae, ma'am. I wondered if you could spare Selina for a few minutes. There's a horse I want to show her."

"I'm certain we can do without her for a bit. I'll get her for you." Lydia turned, then shifted back toward Bram. "Oh, would you like some coffee?"

"Nae, ma'am. I've had plenty this morning." When she hesitated again, he took a slight step forward. "Thought I'd also let you know Bull is doing real good."

Her face brightened. "Is he resting?"

"When he feels the need." It wasn't a lie. So far, Bull hadn't felt the need.

A relieved look passed over her face. "That's good. I'll get Selina for you. Have a seat while you wait."

Chuckling, Bram continued to stand, knowing as soon as Selina heard he wanted to see her, she'd burst through the kitchen door. It happened even faster than he'd guessed.

Seconds later, she rushed up to him, still untying the apron from around her waist. The bright smile, and excited expression, twisted his heart.

In that moment, Bram knew he had to find the nerve to face his feelings. Staring into her sparkling green eyes, he accepted his love for the vivacious, obstinate woman.

"Lydia said you have something to show me."

Her question drew him from thoughts of love for this young woman and back to the reason he'd entered the house. Then his full attention landed on her, and his breath hitched.

He couldn't recall ever seeing her in a dress. Well, except for those occasions he, Thane, and the boys traveled into town for Sunday services. She'd always looked pretty, all gussied up in her best clothes. Today, her radiance drew him in as a fly to honey.

Gripping the brim of his hat tighter, he licked his lips. "Um...aye, lass. One of the mustangs." He struggled to recall what he wanted to show her. "A mustang..." He blinked, confused at his confusion.

Grabbing his hand, she pulled him to the door, stifling a giggle of excitement. "You can tell me outside. Where is he?" Dropping his hand, she rushed to the corral used for breaking the wild horses.

"It's a she. I want to show you one of the mares the ranch hands brought in with a group of mustangs."

Her brows knit together. "While we were gone?"

"Aye. Dax sent out four men to search. They returned with a herd of eight, including their stallion." He knew she'd been looking for an Appaloosa, a rare find in the mustang herds. "Over there." Bram pointed toward an adjoining corral.

Using a hand to block out the sun, her gaze narrowed. He knew the moment when she spotted the mare. Dropping her hand, she moved down the fence line, never shifting her attention from the horse with a dark base blanketed in white, with dark brown spots splattered over its hind quarters.

"She's beautiful." Again, she walked toward the corral holding the mare. "What do you think of her, Bram?"

"She's a sound horse," he replied, his gaze locked on Selina. "Is she what you've been searching for?"

"Exactly. Where did they find the herd?"

"West of here, in the lower mountains. One of them spotted the stallion and followed him. It's a bonny group of horses, lass."

"Yes, it is." Selina studied the mare, pleased with the conformation, the energy and sass when the horse reared back, then kicked her rear hooves in the air. "Do you believe Dax will let me train her for my own?"

Bram had already spoken to him, getting his approval. "He already told me you can have her. But you have to find someone for Honey. Are you ready to give her up?"

Honey had been her horse for most of the time she'd been at the ranch. She loved the spirited mare. Still...

Selina continued to watch the mustang as the animal ran around the corral. Other than Honey, she'd never witnessed a wild mare with such energy, as if she thought herself a stallion.

She inhaled a slow breath. This would be one of the biggest decisions she'd ever made. Honey had been the horse of her youth, a part of her, an animal she'd always love. Could she let her go?

"What are you thinking?" Bram placed a hand on her shoulder, giving a slight squeeze.

"Do I have to make the decision now?"

"Nae, lass. How about you break and gentle her, then make your decision?"

Stepping onto the bottom rail of the fence, she bit her lower lip before licking them. The small gesture caught Bram's attention, his body reacting. A pulsing sensation shot through him, an awareness a man experienced when near a woman he desired. And there'd never been a woman he wanted more than Selina Rinehart.

"All right. I'll start tomorrow." Jumping to the ground, she leaned up, kissing his cheek. The move surprised both of them. "I..."

"It's fine, Selina." Bending down, he brushed a kiss across her cheek. He wanted to do more. Much more, but now wasn't the time or place. Soon, though, she'd understand there wouldn't be another man for her. He'd make certain of it.

The raggedly dressed man sat on a rock high above his dilapidated cabin, mind convulsing in confusion. He didn't understand why the sheriff and a few deputies were searching every inch of what had been his home.

Returning with a full wagon, he'd spotted intruders running down the mountain. Angry, he'd grabbed his rifle, getting off a couple shots. Cursing, he continued to his cabin, surprised to find the friends he made over the last few weeks were gone.

Disheartened, he'd collapsed on the threshold to his home, crying until no more tears fell. He'd experienced loneliness before, but nothing this devastating. Agitated, he'd packed his mule, Dolly, and taken off up the mountain.

He'd returned a few days later to find the sheriff and his men had taken over his home. *His* home. Pulling on his hair at the injustice, he'd stifled a pained shout. They couldn't find him. They could never find him.

Rubbing a hand over his face, he turned to look at his faithful mule. "Dolly, my girl, it's time we moved on. There's no longer anything for us here."

Gabe stood back, fisted hands on hips as he surveyed the cabin. In his opinion, the two room shelter wasn't fit for raccoons, not to mention people. But this is where Amos and Ada had directed them.

Nothing inside pointed to it being where someone had imprisoned three men and two women. Some for days, others for a few weeks. No bindings or straps of leather used to immobilize them. No dirty plates holding dried eggs, as Amos and Ada suggested.

Both were clear about the provisions their abductor had provided. Water, one egg, and bread. Twice a day. He'd provided the food after their use of the privy, feeding them so as not to release the bindings around their wrists. When finished, he'd escorted them back inside, taking out someone else.

"Can't find anything inside, Gabe." Cash left the cabin, wiping dirty hands down his pants, disgust twisting his mouth. "No clothes, supplies, not a darn clue as to who's been living here."

"We know someone has." Beau followed him outside, swiping cobwebs off his hat. "Amos, Ada, and Charley were running down the hill from this location. There aren't any other cabins or shelters close. And it matches their description of the place."

Gabe shook his head, frustrated at the lack of progress or confirmation of a crime. "But there's no sign of habitation."

"Nothing to indicate five people were held against their will." Settling the hat back on his head, Beau joined Gabe and Cash. "There are some piles of donkey or mule dung over at the lean-to." He pointed toward the shelter yards from the cabin.

"Fresh?" Gabe walked up the hill to it, checking for himself.

"Could be several days or weeks old," Beau answered. "Don't know where he'd get the water for an animal, unless he stored snow in something from the winter storms. But there aren't any barrels that I can find."

The western region of the territory had experienced an extreme blizzard at Christmas, raising the water levels in the lakes and rivers to overflowing. Many of the ranchers and some of the townsfolk had filled barrels with snow to use for cooking and drinking.

"We know he lived here," Gabe breathed out. "Must've packed up whatever he owned and left after shooting Winslow." Removing his hat, he scratched his head. "We're missing something. I can feel it."

Cash massaged the back of his neck, then snapped his fingers. "Has anyone talked to Old Will? I'll bet he knows a lot about what goes on in the local mountains."

"Might, but no one knows where he lives." Beau walked back toward what he considered nothing but a shack. "He gets his supplies at Petermann's. Maybe Stan knows where he's been staying." The owner of the general store knew as much about what went on in and around Splendor than anyone.

"Talk to Stan when we get back to town, Beau." Gabe took another look around, stumped at the lack of anything they could use to identify the kidnapper. "Cash, you do the same with Silas at the lumber mill. I'll speak with Noah. Those are the other two places people go for supplies or repairs. Someone has clues about our kidnapper." He glanced between the two. "They just don't know it."

Chapter Twenty-Eight

Splendor

Shane debated whether or not to head to the clinic. He'd stayed away while keeping up on Winslow's condition. According to Georgina, there'd been no improvement, and Doc McCord didn't expect him to survive. Too much blood loss and high fever, indicating an internal infection.

Guilt about leaving Angela to worry all alone ate at him. When young, he'd spent too many years being her protector, keeping the bullies away, as well as those with a real interest in the budding beauty. Both equally dangerous to his young heart. Shane couldn't seem to leave his compulsion to watch over her in the past.

Cursing under his breath, he accepted he couldn't stay away. If Winslow died, Shane wanted someone besides a nurse to be with her.

Carrying food from the boardinghouse, he walked the short distance to the clinic. The lamps still burned inside, emitting a welcoming glow to the sick and injured.

Climbing the steps, he shoved open the door to see Angela in the same chair as the last time he'd seen her. Back straight, hands clasped in her lap, eyes locked on the door separating her from Winslow, his heart constricted. After all this time, he still loved her.

The sound of the door closing had her shifting to look at him. Her expression didn't change. The only movement was the rise and fall of her chest.

"Have you eaten?" He held up the wrapped food. Her lips pressed together as she shrugged. "You have to eat, Angela. When he gets better, he'll need your strength."

"He isn't going to get better, Shane." Letting out a breath, she seemed to retreat into herself.

Setting down the food, he sat next to her, prying her hands apart to take one in his. "I'm sorry. If there was something I could do..." He let the thought hang between them.

"He wasn't my choice, but Carson is a good man. I know he'd do anything for me." Sad eyes met his concerned ones. "I'm not good enough for him."

Anger flowed through him at the comment. He might never trust her again, never had the opportunity to express his rage about the lie her father had told, but he wouldn't allow her to disparage herself.

Gripping her shoulders, he turned her to face him. "Any man would be honored to have you as his wife, Angela."

Her sad gaze flinched at the ire in his. "Including you, Shane?"

Dropping his hands, he stood, looking away. "Anyone except me. Not only are you engaged to someone else, but we had our chance. It's too late for us now, Angela."

Her throat worked as she processed his answer. Profound despair distorted her features, making him feel as if he'd taken away her last book. When young, nothing had been more important to Angela than her small library consisting of a dozen books and dime novels. As he recalled, the pages were worn from being read over and over.

Taking his seat again, he leaned back, crossing his arms. "I'm sorry if my answer seems harsh."

Reaching out, she touched his arm before drawing her hand away. "What I've never understood is why you left me.

Eyes wide in disbelief, he opened his mouth to deny it, stopping when the door to Winslow's room opened. Clay walked out, closing the distance between them, his features grim.

Shane held out his hand, assisting Angela up. "How is he, Doctor?"

Glancing at Shane, Clay gave an almost imperceptible shake of his head. "I'm afraid it's not good news. Would you prefer to sit down?"

Back rigid, she held her ground. "No. Please just tell me how he's doing."

Shane wanted to loop an arm over her shoulders, provide some measure of support. Knowing he didn't have the right, he didn't move.

"I'm sorry, Miss Baldwin. The internal damage from the bullet was too extensive. I couldn't save him."

Her face drained of color, body swayed a moment before her eyes rolled back in her head.

"Angela!" Shane grabbed her before she landed on the floor.

Scooping her into his arms, he followed Clay to a room with a bed. Placing her in the center, he took the blanket from Clay's outstretched hand, covering her from neck to toes. Opening a cupboard, Clay picked up a small bottle, opening the lid, he waved it under her nose.

"Smelling salts," he explained to Shane as they waited for Angela to react. It didn't take long.

Inhaling, she jerked her head away. "What..."

"Relax, Angela. You fainted."

"Fainted? I..." Then she remembered the doctor's words. "Carson," she whispered, her eyes closing for a few painful seconds before opening. "He's gone."

Shane stroked the back of her hand, wishing he could take away her anguish. "Yes."

The first tear rolled down her face, followed by more until she rolled away. Covering her face, her quiet sobs broke his heart. He wanted to hold her, tell her everything would be all right, but as before, he had no right.

"I'll leave you two alone. Let me know if she wants to say her goodbyes." Clay stepped into the waiting room, closing the door behind him.

Sitting on the edge of the bed, he rested a hand on her shoulder. Shane already knew what would come next.

Clay would prepare the body to be placed in a casket for transportation back to Boston. Angela would board the train, wave a final goodbye, and Shane's heart would break for a second time.

Billy shot another glance down the long table where Shining Star sat holding Spirit Bear. She'd been sullen since the group returned, learning Bull had spent a few days recovering in the Blackfoot village. It was as if a light had gone out in her eyes.

He understood. A white man was welcome, but she and her child were not. The knowledge was a cruel blow to a young woman who'd been through so much.

Supper, meant to be a celebration of Bull's recovery, had been more subdued than Billy expected. Bull didn't enjoy the attention, but would never ruin Lydia's excitement. The women had worked since early morning to offer a lavish meal for him.

When Dax stood, signaling the end of the formal meal, Billy waited as the others rose to congregate in the living room. He continued to wait while the women collected the dishes, taking them into the kitchen.

Alone at the table with Shining Star, he closed the distance between them, taking a sleeping Spirit Bear from her arms. On a normal night, the baby would be secured to her chest while she helped the women clean. The deep sadness he saw cut through him.

Until Bull's wound, she'd held out hope her brother and grandfather would return to take her home. The slim amount of hope had evaporated. At least, that was what Billy believed.

He'd believed they were growing closer, that she might love him enough to want to remain at the ranch. Billy now understood she'd always want to return to her village.

"Billy Zales?" The tremble in her voice had him grabbing a chair to sit next to her.

"Yes?"

"Can we go home now?"

Had he heard her right? "If you're ready to leave, I'll walk you to your house."

"You do not understand. I want you to go home with me."

Lips parting, he stared into clear, brown eyes sparkling with a hope he hadn't expected. He grasped what she was offering him. Unlike the other times he'd been inside her house, if he walked into her home tonight, she'd have the expectation they would marry.

"Do you know what you're asking me, Shining Star?"

A slight blush crept up her cheeks. Reaching out, she covered his hand with hers. "Yes, I understand."

Heart pounding, a lump grew in his throat. He had a decision to make, and little time to make it. Standing, he adjusted the baby in his arms before holding out a hand to help her up.

"Let's take a walk."

Fingers entwined, he led her through the living room, ignoring the odd looks from the others. Outside, he headed toward the corral where the wild mustangs grazed.

Billy couldn't imagine ever leaving Redemption's Edge. Over the years, it had become a part of him, was in his blood and his heart. Much the same as Shining Star and Spirit Bear. The decision had been easier than he imagined.

Turning to face her, he bent down, giving her time to back away before brushing his lips across hers. When she didn't move, he slipped his free hand behind her neck, settling his mouth on hers for a longer, more intense kiss. After a moment, Billy raised his head.

"I love you, Shining Star." Brushing one more light kiss across her lips, he stepped away. "I would be honored to enter your house."

"I'm glad you were able to stay for supper, Bram. There's room for you and Thane if you don't want to ride back to your ranch tonight." Dax handed him a shot of whiskey, watching the activities continue through the open doors of his study.

"We might do that." Taking a sip of his drink, he walked to the window offering a view of the barn, corrals, and mountains beyond. The ranch was magnificent, as much so as Circle M.

"Thanks to help from you and Thane, Luke and I signed another Army contract while you were at Fort Connall. This one is to provide horses for Fort Laramie and some neighboring posts." Dax leaned a hip against his desk. "It's for a minimum of four dozen horses."

Bram almost choked on his whiskey. "Forty-eight horses?"

"At minimum. It's a little late to ask, but can we do it?"

Chuckling, yet humbled at Dax's confidence in his men, Bram lowered himself into one of the overstuffed chairs. "Aye. When does the Army require them?"

"First of August. A fair amount of time."

"Aye, it is." Rolling the glass between his fingers, Bram stared at the contents.

Four dozen horses would mean working from sunup to sunset six days a week. It also meant the herd would have to consist of a majority of wild horses. Rubbing his jaw, Bram considered the reason he wanted to meet with Dax, which had nothing to do with Army contracts.

"I've already talked to Bull and Dirk about rounding up more mustangs. They're certain we'll have to ride farther into the mountains to get enough."

"We'll be needing at least fifty-five to sixty horses to meet the agreement."

Dax took the chair next to Bram, brows bunching together. "They prefer geldings, but will accept strong mares."

"Will they take stallions? I'd rather not geld the herd leaders."

"Agreed. Splitting the stallions between your ranch and ours is my preference." Dax tapped his glass on the arm of his chair, shifting when the door opened. "Luke, come in. We're discussing the Army contract."

"Quite the deal, don't you think, Bram?" Luke poured himself a drink, taking the bottle with him as he took a seat on the sofa across from the others.

"Aye. Challenging, but I've no doubt we can fulfill it. The concern is, we've all been wanting to grow our breeding programs. This will leave us little time for that."

Luke looked at Dax. "Maybe we should hire more men to work with the herd. That would free up Bull and Tad. We'd leave Dirk ramrodding the cattle. The two newest ranch hands have more experience with wild horses than most of our hands."

"Could work," Dax said. "How about you, Bram? Are you able to hire more men?"

"Aye. Assuming we can find some good ones. Kev and Vince will be in charge while Thane and I are here."

Dax nodded. "They're pretty young."

"I've seen few men who work as hard as those two. The lads are also smart." Bram finished the last of his whiskey. Setting the glass down, he stood. "I've something else to talk to you about." Moving behind the chair, he rested his hands on the back.

Dax stretched out his legs, crossing them at the ankles. "What is that?"

"I intend to marry Selina."

Chapter Twenty-Nine

Not much surprised Dax or Luke. By the look on their faces, Bram had managed to shock them.

"Selina?" Luke set down his half-full glass, leaning forward. "Have you lost your mind?"

A grin curved Bram's lips. "Aye, it's possible I've gone daft."

Dax drew his legs in to stand. "I can't say I'm surprised."

Luke's mouth gaped open. "Are you daft, too?"

Eyes crinkling with mirth, Dax grinned. "Maybe. Still, I've seen how Selina has changed since working with Bram. She's more responsible."

"Such as running off to ride with the herd to Fort Connall?" Luke challenged.

Dax shrugged off his brother's concern. "We've already dealt with her disappearing." He looked at Bram. "Do you realize how much work it will be if you marry Selina? She's demanding, willful, stubborn, and impulsive. She cares nothing about running a house. Do you even know if she wants children?"

Straightening, Bram picked up his glass, filling it with whiskey. "I know the lass is smart, caring, and loyal. Selina would do anything for her family, which is everyone on the ranch. She works hard, and is passionate about breeding horses." Taking a sip, he waited for the heat of the amber liquid to hit his belly. "We've lots of time to decide about a family."

"I expect you'll live on your ranch," Dax said.

"Aye. She'll ride with us back here each day. If there are times she wants to stay over, I won't stop her."

Luke nodded his understanding. "Do you love her?"

"I do."

"Then there's not much else to say." Picking up the bottle, Luke topped off their glasses, holding his up. "Best of luck to you, Bram. I don't have to tell you how much you'll need it."

Bram found Selina by the corral where the wild mare grazed. She stood on the lowest rail, arms crossed on the top, her chin resting on them. Still wearing the dress and scuffed boots, she seemed lost in thought.

Stopping several yards away, he watched her stare at the mare, as if she had a difficult decision to make. Which he knew she did.

Bram had faced the same choice years earlier when he'd decided to keep Bullet—a gelding he'd bred and trained. Instead of selling his first horse, a gelding years older than Bullet, the family kept him at the ranch for use by the younger children. He believed Dax and Luke would do the same if Selina kept the younger mare.

He didn't know how much time passed before she dropped to the ground, turned, and froze. A slow smile spread across her face when she spotted Bram.

"How long have you been there?"

"Not long." His gaze roamed over her, taking in every detail. "You appeared to be deep in thought."

Turning back toward the corral, she sighed. "I was."

"Because you keep the mare for yourself doesn't mean you will lose Honey. Consider how many lads and lasses are growing up on the ranch. It won't be long until they will be begging to have their first horse."

She looked up at him, eyes wide. "Honey would be a perfect choice."

"Aye, she would."

"Thank you, Bram." Looping her arm through his, she tugged him toward the corral. "I still must ask Dax if I'm allowed to work with the horses tomorrow."

Glancing down at her, he couldn't stop warmth from spreading through him. He hadn't expected her to latch onto him as if they were a couple. They were, but he hadn't explained that part to her yet. By her actions, he would make that clear soon.

"I doubt he'll keep you from them any longer. If you want, I'll ask him for you."

She was quiet for a moment before looking up at him. "No. I must speak with him myself."

One corner of Bram's mouth tipped up, pride shining in his eyes.

"Perhaps I should do it now, before he retreats for the night."

"Tomorrow will be soon enough, Selina. Please join me for a walk."

"A walk sounds much better than talking to Dax. You're right. Tomorrow will be fine."

Placing a hand over hers, he headed to the far edge of the corral, both watching the Appaloosa. "It's rare to find such a fine animal in a herd of mustangs. She's a treasure." Bram looked at her. "A perfect horse for you."

Her heart stuttered at the intense look on his face. This was what she'd hoped for, being alone with Bram, having him look at her as if she were the only woman for miles.

He stopped, glancing up. "We have beautiful night skies at our ranch in California. But these..." Bram raised his head again, letting out a slow breath. "These are magnificent. I've never seen skies such a midnight blue, with stars that go on forever."

"Why, I do believe you are a poet, Mr. MacLaren."

A bark of laughter followed her comment. "If there's one thing I'm not, it's a poet." He faced her, one arm slipping around her waist. It was a bold move, one he hoped she'd allow. When she didn't pull away, he brushed hair from her face, cupping her cheek. "You've been a surprise, lass."

"Surprise?"

"Aye. I came all this way to expand our ranch, breed and train horses. What I didn't expect was to find a lass as intriguing as you."

Selina's lips parted, her breathing becoming erratic. "I'm a simple ranch woman."

"Nae. You are far from simple." Lifting her chin with a finger, he bent his head down to within inches of her lips. "I'm going to kiss you, lass."

Gripping his arms, she raised her face toward him. "Yes."

Closing the distance, he took her mouth in a soft, searching kiss. It wasn't chaste or tentative. The claiming left no doubt of his intent, how much he desired her. Lifting his head, he stared into glassy eyes.

"Don't stop," she whispered.

He couldn't hold back a chuckle. "Ah, lass. I've no intention of stopping. Not ever."

The couple stayed in the dark for a long time, embracing, kissing, until one of her legs began rubbing up and down his. Bram knew the time had come to return her to the house. After one last kiss, he stepped away.

"We should go back, lass." His voice was thick, as if it was hard to get the sentence out.

Selina glanced down, smoothing the wrinkles from her dress. "I don't want to."

"Neither do I. If we don't, Dax may send men out to find us." Taking a calming breath, he took her hands in his. "Besides, I've something to say on our walk back."

She prayed he didn't tell her tonight had been a mistake, never to be repeated. Could their closeness feel so right to her, but not for him? She hoped not.

Dropping one hand, he continued to grip the other, entwining their fingers. "Our ranch on the other side of Splendor isn't much. Thane and I have two hands, and we plan to hire more. We're here most days, but there will come a time when we'll have to be at our own place more often."

Selina wondered where this was headed, but ignored her urge to ask.

"It will take time, but someday, our ranch in Montana will be as large as the one in California." Bram looked over at her, seeing her staring at him. "Am I speaking gibberish?"

She tightened her hold on his hand, anxious for him to continue. "Not at all. I want to know all about your ranch, and your plans."

Bending down, he brushed his lips across hers, then smiled. "We'll run cattle and breed horses. Much the same as here, but we'll spend more time on the horses."

"Will you still work with Dax and Luke?"

"We plan to, although a good deal of work will be done at our ranch. We won't need to be on the trail so much, which will free up our time." Lifting their joined hands, he kissed her knuckles. Slowing their pace, he stopped, facing her.

"This is all new to me, lass. What I'm trying to say is, I want you to be with me as we grow the ranch."

Cocking her head, she raised a brow. "You want me to work with you at your ranch instead of here?"

Closing his eyes, he fought for the right words. "Nae, lass. What I want is for you to share it with me. By my side, as my wife."

Eyes wide, she took a step back, a hand settling over her heart. "Your...wife?"

"Aye." Chest squeezing, he noted how pale her face had gone. He was doing this all wrong. "Maybe this is a conversation for another time."

Swallowing, her hand reached out to cup his cheek. "No, please explain what's in your head."

"If you're sure."

Nodding, she lowered her hand to take his. "Yes."

"It won't be easy. Long hours, hard work. You'll work with the horses every day, either here or at our ranch. There will be no end to what you learn."

"You'd marry me to help grow the horse business. I'm not sure that's a good reason to tie yourself to a woman. Or for me to commit to a man."

It was Bram's turn to show surprise. "Nae, it would be a bad idea to marry for just the horses."

"Then tell me why I should marry you." Heart pounding inside her chest, her breathing came in short gasps.

The confusion cleared from his features as he understood. Cupping her face with both hands, he locked his gaze with hers.

"We should marry because I love you, lass. Do you feel the same for me?" Holding his breath, he sent up a prayer he was right.

Relief washed through her. Selina had known what she felt for Bram was love. Deep, intense, and all-consuming. And he felt the same.

"Lass?"

A broad smile brightened her face as tears pooled in her eyes. "I love you, too, Bram. Yes, I'll marry you."

Flinging her arms around him, he buried his face against her neck. Through ragged breaths, he lifted his mouth against her ear. "Not a day will go by you won't feel loved."

"I know, Bram. I know..."

Epilogue

Redemption's Edge
Two weeks later...

"They're such a perfect couple, don't you think so, Bram?"

Tightening his hold around Selina's waist, he grinned, watching the newlyweds talk with Bull and Lydia. The couple had made the decision to have the ceremony and celebration at the ranch. Reverend and Mrs. Paige had been happy to ride out, the back of their wagon filled with food and flowers.

"Yes. Shining Star made a good decision." He chuckled when she slapped his arm.

"Don't you mean Billy? He finally came to his senses and told her how he felt."

A grin tugged at Bram's lips. "Let's agree they both made the right decision."

Several days had passed since Selina and Bram had announced their intention to marry. They'd been holding hands when the living room quieted in stunned silence for several seconds before Rachel jumped up, hugging both of them. The others soon followed.

At the MacLaren ranch, Kev and Vince had taken the news with indifference. Neither had met Selina, and couldn't see a reason to show any reaction other than shaking Bram's hand. Thane had slapped them on their backs, laughing as the two strolled away to continue their work.

The reaction from the Circle M in California had been different. Telegrams flew between Splendor and Conviction, the closest town to the MacLaren ranch. The last correspondence Bram received indicated a small group of family planned to attend the wedding.

"Have you two set a date for your wedding?" Griffin MacKenzie, Bram's longtime friend who they'd followed from California, bent to brush a chaste kiss on Selina's cheek. "Heard the family may be coming out."

"The telegraph arrived late yesterday. How'd you hear about it, Griff?"

"Thane. He's excited to see them." Leaning closer, he lowered his voice. "The boy's missing his ma, Quinn, Lara, and Bryce."

Bram thought of his mother and siblings, a lump building deep in his throat. He missed them, too.

Selina looked between the two men, feeling fortunate her family and friends were all in Splendor. "We'd thought of having the wedding soon, but I believe we should put it off until we know when Bram's family can arrive."

"June fifteenth. We'll not put it off any farther."

Selina gasped at the date. "That's just a month away, Bram. Will they have enough time to get here?"

Griffin rubbed the back of his neck. "She's right, Bram. Even if you notify them Monday of the date, they won't have enough time."

Mouth twisting into a scowl, he counted the days. "June twenty-ninth. That's as far as I'll go. In fact, it's a month longer than I want to wait." The disgust in his voice had Selina and Griffin stifling laughter.

"I'll speak with Reverend Paige about the date." Selina kissed Bram's cheek before heading toward a group which included the Paiges.

Griffin pulled a flask from the inside pocket of his coat, holding it out to Bram. "Are you sure about this?"

Taking a sip, his brows furrowed. "About marrying Selina?"

"You haven't known her long. From what I know, she's nothing like the women you were attracted to in Conviction."

Features hardening, his words were clipped, boarding on irritation. "I never courted any of them."

Holding up his hands, Griffin shook his head. "No offense. I felt the question needed to be asked. Must be the lawyer in me."

Bram's gaze moved across the room to where Selina was speaking with Rachel and Dax. "You don't know her the way I do." Taking one more slow sip of whiskey, he handed the flask back to Griffin. "Aye, I'm certain."

Clasping him on the shoulder, Griffin gave a light squeeze. "I'm happy for you, Bram. Don't think for a moment I'm not."

Shifting to meet his friend's sincere gaze, Bram held out his hand. "Thanks, lad."

Across the room, several deputies stood together with their wives, talking about the kidnapping. Gabe took a swallow of his drink, his gut telling him the person responsible may have left the area after the shooting.

"No one's seen Old Will since before Amos, Ada, and Charley escaped," Gabe said. "The cabin where they were held was empty. Nothing to indicate anyone was ever there. We don't even know if that's where Old Will lived."

"Do you think he's the one who took them and killed Winslow, Gabe?" Mack Mackey asked.

"I don't know. From the little I know about him, Old Will has never come across as a killer...or a kidnapper. He might be a little off in the head, but the rest? Makes no sense. The problem is, he's disappeared."

The others nodded, knowing all they could do was continue to search for a man who'd abducted five people and killed one.

Several feet away, Shane Banderas held a cup of punch, his features unreadable.

"I heard Miss Baldwin left." His good friend, Hawke DeBell, a newlywed himself, had come up beside him.

"Yesterday. She's returning to Boston."

Hawke's gaze narrowed. "What about Winslow's body?"

"Mrs. Winslow sent a telegram saying she was sending people out to bring the remains home." Shane couldn't hide the disgust in his voice. "Doesn't matter to me.

However, the family wants to take care of the body is none of my business."

Hawke could hear the lie in Shane's voice. He might not care about Winslow, but his friend still cared a great deal about Angela Baldwin.

Thank you for taking the time to read Paradise Point. If you enjoyed it, please consider telling your friends or posting a short review. Word of mouth is an author's best friend and much appreciated.

Watch for book eighteen in the Redemption Mountain series, **_Silent Sunset_**.

If you want in on all the backstage action of my historical westerns, join my VIP Readers Group.

Join my Newsletter to be notified of Pre-Orders and New Releases:
https://www.shirleendavies.com/

I care about quality, so if you find an error, please contact me via email at
shirleen@shirleendavies.com

About the Author

Shirleen Davies writes romance. She is the best-selling author of books in the romantic suspense, military romance, historical western romance, and contemporary western romance genres. Shirleen grew up in Southern California, attended Oregon State University, and has degrees from San Diego State University and the University of Maryland. Her passion is writing emotionally charged stories of flawed people who find redemption through love and acceptance. She lives with her husband in a beautiful town in northern Arizona.

I love to hear from my readers!

Send me an email: shirleen@shirleendavies.com
Visit my Website: https://www.shirleendavies.com/
Sign up to be notified of New Releases:
https://www.shirleendavies.com/
Follow me on Amazon:
http://www.amazon.com/author/shirleendavies
Follow me on BookBub:
https://www.bookbub.com/authors/shirleen-davies

Other ways to connect with me:

Facebook Author Page:
http://www.facebook.com/shirleendaviesauthor
Twitter: www.twitter.com/shirleendavies
Pinterest: http://pinterest.com/shirleendavies
Instagram:
https://www.instagram.com/shirleendavies_author/

Books by Shirleen Davies

Historical Western Romance Series
Redemption Mountain

Redemption's Edge, Book One
Wildfire Creek, Book Two
Sunrise Ridge, Book Three
Dixie Moon, Book Four
Survivor Pass, Book Five
Promise Trail, Book Six
Deep River, Book Seven
Courage Canyon, Book Eight
Forsaken Falls, Book Nine
Solitude Gorge, Book Ten
Rogue Rapids, Book Eleven
Angel Peak, Book Twelve
Restless Wind, Book Thirteen
Storm Summit, Book Fourteen
Mystery Mesa, Book Fifteen
Thunder Valley, Book Sixteen
A Very Splendor Christmas, Holiday Novella, Book Seventeen
Paradise Point, Book Eighteen,
Silent Sunset, Book Nineteen, Coming Next in the Series!

MacLarens of Boundary Mountain

Colin's Quest, Book One,
Brodie's Gamble, Book Two
Quinn's Honor, Book Three
Sam's Legacy, Book Four

Heather's Choice, Book Five
Nate's Destiny, Book Six
Blaine's Wager, Book Seven
Fletcher's Pride, Book Eight
Bay's Desire, Book Nine
Cam's Hope, Book Ten

MacLarens of Fire Mountain

Tougher than the Rest, Book One
Faster than the Rest, Book Two
Harder than the Rest, Book Three
Stronger than the Rest, Book Four
Deadlier than the Rest, Book Five
Wilder than the Rest, Book Six

Romantic Suspense

Eternal Brethren, Military Romantic Suspense

Steadfast, Book One
Shattered, Book Two
Haunted, Book Three
Untamed, Book Four
Devoted, Book Five
Faithful, Book Six
Exposed, Book Seven
Undaunted, Book Eight
Resolute, Book Nine
Unspoken, Book Ten, Coming Next in the Series!

Peregrine Bay, Romantic Suspense

Reclaiming Love, Book One
Our Kind of Love, Book Two
Edge of Love, Book Three, Coming Next in the Series!

<u>*Contemporary Romance Series*</u>

MacLarens of Fire Mountain

Second Summer, Book One
Hard Landing, Book Two
One More Day, Book Three
All Your Nights, Book Four
Always Love You, Book Five
Hearts Don't Lie, Book Six
No Getting Over You, Book Seven
'Til the Sun Comes Up, Book Eight
Foolish Heart, Book Nine

Macklin's of Burnt River

Thorn's Journey
Del's Choice
Boone's Surrender

The best way to stay in touch is to subscribe to my newsletter. Go to https://www.shirleendavies.com/ and subscribe in the box at the top of the right column that asks for your email. You'll be notified of new books before they are released, have chances to win great prizes, and receive other subscriber-only specials.